# *The* Woman *with* Golden Hair

## Phoebe's Third Mystery

Sydney Tooman Betts

All Scriptures quoted are from the King James Version of the Bible.

*The Woman with Golden Hair* is entirely a work of fiction. Any similarity to actual events or people, including peerage, is purely coincidental except for historical figures and a few portrayals written with permission.

Cover design by Anita Thubakabra Mihalyi

ISBN 978-1-7329079-5-9

*In honor of the real*

***Mary and Gary Nelson***

*I am grateful for the decades of love and support*

*they have offered to my husband, children, and me*

Other series by
Sydney Tooman Betts

**The People of the Book**

*A River Too Deep*

*Light Bird's Song*

*Straight Flies the Arrow*

**Phoebe's Mysteries**

*Phoebe's Secret*

*Phoebe's Christmas*

*The Woman with Golden Hair*

# Characters

## The Farrells

**Ernest**: a northern pastor in a southern town
**Amelia:** Ernest's wife
**Phoebe:** Ernest and Amelia's eighteen-year-old daughter
**August:** Phoebe's nine-year-old brother
**Lucy:** Ernest and Amelia's late-in-life surprise
**Foster**: the church and parsonage gardener and caretaker

## The Kikers

**Asa:** owner of The Lilacs, a local rye plantation
**Lavinia:** Asa's elegant and headstrong wife
**Hugh:** Asa and Lavinia's dark-haired, dark-eyed son
**Clara:** Asa and Lavinia's daughter, Hugh's sister
**Mitilde:** the Kikers' enslaved cook
**Kitch**: Mitilde's husband and The Lilacs' under foreman
**Jubal**: Mitilde's nephew who acts as a butler and coachman
**Sari**: an observant houseslave

## The Nelsons

**Gary:** a former colonel who has befriended the Farrells
**Mary:** Gary's lovely and gracious wife
**Emily:** The Nelson's granddaughter and Phoebe's friend

### The Simmonses

**Mahala:** the widowed matriarch of the Simmons family
**Charles:** Mahala's eldest son and Hugh Kiker's oldest friend
**William:** Charles's slightly younger brother
**Virginia:** Mahala's eldest daughter and Clara Kiker's friend
**Megan:** Virginia's seventeen-year-old sister
**Jeremiah:** Augie's eight-year-old playmate
**Sarah:** Mahala's thoughtful youngest daughter
**Ruby**: the Simmonses' housekeeper and Mitilde's sister

### The Wilsons and Whites

**Allison:** Alcy Callen's girlhood friend from *A River too Deep*
**John:** Allison's husband who is as tall as a tree
**Lisa White:** the Wilsons' daughter and Phoebe's friend
**Jordan White:** Lisa's husband
**Jack**: the Whites' toddling son

### The Guests

**Isabela:** a woman who is lost
**Aaron Auger:** a visitor from Pennsylvania
**Alan Dyer:** an investigator who is acquainted with Phoebe
**Wesley Pinder**: an English guest at The Lilacs
**Richard Whitcomb:** another English visitor

# Chapter 1

October 6, 1844

WHILE REVEREND FARRELL leaned closer to his birthday candles, the light shimmered off the strands of silver sprinkling his black hair. Sixteen months ago, they merely peppered his temples. Perhaps the progression was natural, thought his daughter, Phoebe, but she feared their move to the Shenandoah Valley had taken its toll. Not only was he a northern pastor opposed to southern policies, but he had also stumbled upon two murders. The first victim headed one family in his church and worked for another. The second was a stranger. At least Papa had learned nothing of her employer's secret.

As Phoebe passed a slice of cake to Gary Nelson, the church's head deacon, she wondered how much he knew. He could easily be a conspirator. He eschewed slavery and certainly had the aptitude. During the War for Independence, he had been a spy, subsequently rising to the rank of colonel. However, though he and his wife, Mary, were like grandparents to her, she dared not ask.

While she cut another slice, she considered Emily, the Nelsons' *actual* granddaughter and her closest friend. Em was aware of something. She had let a hint slip after Phoebe had voiced qualms about working at a plantation, though she had not caught Emily's full meaning until much later.

"Mrs. Nelson, would you like a piece?"

"Yes, but those two are too large. I'll pass them to Emily and your little brother."

"Is this small enough?"

"Perfect."

Mary Nelson might be an even better candidate than the colonel. Apart from age, were someone to describe her superficially, the listener might confuse her with Phoebe's mother. Both had blue eyes and brown hair, though Mary's was now strewn with white. Both avidly followed Jesus, and both made everyone around them feel welcome. Still, that was where the similarity stopped. Mama resembled a barnyard hen, dithering endearingly over all within her realm. Mrs. Nelson was a poised and unflappable swan. Perhaps, all three Nelsons were involved.

Emily's laughter drew her attention. She was teasing Augie, Phoebe's nine-year-old brother, who had smeared icing through his dark curls while feeding cake to Sparkles, his dog.

"Do you hear that, Ernest?" Mama laid down her dessert fork as the retriever bounded toward the front door.

"Hear what, Amelia?"

"That scratching."

Above the clicking of the dog's nails, they listened for the faint sound.

Colonel Nelson lifted an eyebrow toward his thinning hairline. "If I couldn't see Sparkles from where I sit, I'd say he was wanting to come in."

Reverend Farrell scraped his chair backward, signaling for Augie to sit down. "No need for us both to go, son. I'll see who it is."

"You can help me clear," suggested Phoebe, "unless anyone would like another piece of Papa's birthday cake. Emily?"

"No. It was delicious, but I've had plenty. I'll help you wash the…."

"Amelia!" The reverend shouted from the foyer. "You'd better come."

As his wife rushed from the table, Phoebe and Emily plunked down the plates and followed. A woman, framed in the parsonage doorway, was lying on the porch.

"Oh, the poor dear." Amelia knelt to find the stranger's pulse and feel her forehead. "She doesn't have a fever, Ernest. If you and Gary will lift her onto the settee, Mary and I can loosen her stays." She glanced over her shoulder at Mrs. Nelson, who was just behind Emily and Phoebe, while Augie pushed past all three.

"Is she dead?"

"No, Augie." His sister rolled her eyes, brown like their father's, up at the ceiling. "If she were, Mama and Mrs. Nelson wouldn't need to untie her corset."

"Who made you the expert?"

Phoebe nudged him aside while Reverend Farrell and Colonel Nelson hefted the woman up and carried her to the parlor. "Mama, how can I help?"

"Fetch my smelling salts. Augie, go upstairs and find a blanket. Unconscious or not, she will not want us gawking at her undergarments. And please be careful not to wake the baby."

Emily crouched beside the settee. "What can I do, Grandmother?"

"Your young fingers are nimbler than mine. See all those tiny buttons running down her bodice? If you would start undoing them from the bottom while Mrs. Farrell works her way down from the top, we can reach her stays more quickly. She needs to breathe."

"What do you think happened?"

"I don't know, Emily. Amelia, do you think she fainted?"

"I'm not sure. She is so thin; I wouldn't be surprised if she passed out from hunger."

Reverend Farrell handed his wife the smelling salts his daughter passed to him, but though she waved them beneath the stranger's well-shaped nose, they did nothing to rouse her. "She's rather young. I'd venture less than a decade older than the girls. Gary, you've lived in this valley far longer than we have. Is she at all familiar to you?"

Colonel Nelson shook his head. "She's not from these parts. Perhaps one of the settlements north of Winchester or south toward Staunton. Mary, do you recognize her?"

"No. Her clothing is too fine for a farmer's wife, and see her hands? I doubt they've seen a day's toil."

Augie held out the blanket. "How'd she end up here, Papa?"

"I would imagine she spotted the church, and when no one answered there, she noticed our lights up the hill."

"But why would she be wanderin' around the countryside? There's nothin' but farmland in every direction."

"Good question." The colonel laid his hand on the boy's shoulder. "It's an awfully long way to walk."

Augie squinted up at him. "Maybe she was ridin' a horse. I'll see if I can find one."

"Wherever she came from," answered Amelia, "she's in no condition to return. Ernest, where shall we put her?"

The reverend shrugged. "How about your room, Phoebe? Would you mind bunking with your brother?" When she did not answer, he saw she and Emily had followed Augie outside and were scouring the shrubs abutting the walkway.

A few minutes later, Augie hurried through the open door. "Nope. No horse or carriage."

"Thank you for looking. Very odd. Here, son, please carry this candle to the girls."

Augie did, grabbing another for himself. "What are we searching for, Phebes?"

"Her reticule. She wasn't wearing one on her wrist, so we thought she might have dropped it."

Colonel Nelson popped his head outside. "Find anything?"

"No, sir." They returned to the walkway and stepped inside just as Augie and Phoebe's father was reaching for his hat. "Papa, where are you going?"

"To fetch Dr. Stillman."

"You won't find him. Mary, Emily, and I dropped off some corn at his place earlier. His wife said he's tending to a difficult delivery in Strasburg and didn't expect him home until tomorrow."

"Gary," called Mary from the foyer. "The woman isn't injured. Why don't we take her home with *us*? We can make her comfortable in the carriage, and we'll be closer to the doctor when he breaks free."

"It's fine with me. What do you two think?"

"Frankly," answered Amelia, "I'd find that a relief. Between baby Lucy, Phoebe, and Augie, we really haven't the room. What do you say, dear?"

"It's an excellent plan. Here, Mary, let me help you up."

"Thank you, Ernest. These old knees are not what they used to be." After she was on her feet, she brushed the curls back from the stranger's face. "I wish we at least knew what to call her."

Augie smiled. "Her golden hair's so thick, it's straight out of a fairy-tale. Let's call her Rapunzel."

"Perhaps something a little less extraordinary."

"Isabela! Like the queen."

"All right, Augie," Mrs. Nelson agreed. "Isabela it is."

# Chapter 2

AS PHOEBE DROVE into The Lilacs, she waved at the towering ebony man ambling in her direction. "Good morning, Kitch."

"Morning, Missy Phoebe. Missus Lavinia said you was to fetch'er the moment you came. She's in 'er writin' room." He patted the parsonage horse on the neck. "I'll take care of Esmerelda."

"Thank you." Climbing down from the wagon, Phoebe gathered her skirts, ran up the tall front steps, crossed the wide veranda, and entered the gray stone plantation house.

"Mrs. Kiker?" she knocked on the door of her employer's study.

"Come on in."

"I'm sorry I'm late." Phoebe stepped into the tiny writing room, as tastefully fitted-out as the dark-haired woman behind the desk. "We had some excitement at the parsonage last night, and afterward, I couldn't sleep."

"Never you mind, and wipe that frown from your pretty little forehead. You'll give yourself wrinkles. Ask Mitilde to make us some fresh coffee, then we can get started on today's correspondence."

"Yes, ma'am." Phoebe noticed an unusual amount of busyness between the dining room and parlor. While ducking into the kitchen, she wondered if the reason was connected to Mrs. Kiker's convivial spirits. "Mitilde? Would you have time to make Mrs. Kiker and me some coffee?"

"Land o' Mercy, child. What difference is me havin' time gonna make? I gots more to do than a skunk in a hen-house." She stopped when she noticed Phoebe's dimples fading. "Don't pay me no mind. An' any way, it's all happy doin's. Master Hugh's comin' home."

The grin that spread across the dark face set Phoebe's cheeks to creasing again. Though she hated to see anyone enslaved, she'd grown to love The Lilacs' cook and had missed Hugh more than she expected. "When?"

"Don't know 'xactly, but you go on now an' 'tend to Missus' Lavinia's letters. I'll fetch you that coffee shortly."

No wonder Mrs. Kiker seemed so happy. As Phoebe rounded the door to the hallway, she nearly smacked straight into Hugh's sister.

"There you are!" Clara twisted a dark curl around one of her fingers. "Mother asked me to bring you outside where it's cooler. I've heard you had quite a time last evening."

Phoebe was as surprised by her affability as she was by the remark. Though they enjoyed the same circle of friends, Clara had always shown her a marked lack of interest. Perhaps she considered Phoebe too young to be an intimate or felt she was socially inferior. The Kikers *were* the leading local family; Phoebe was just a pastor's daughter—and an employee. Nonetheless, Mrs. Kiker wished for her to cultivate the relationship. How she had already heard about the woman on their doorstep, Phoebe could not imagine. "Yes, the poor woman. So young to be…so alone."

"I swear, Phoebe, you do talk in riddles."

"But you just…"

"Land sakes, Clara," called her mother. "What's keeping the two of you?"

"We're coming." She clutched Phoebe's arm and pulled her through the door to the veranda.

Lavinia was sitting at a white wicker table, holding up a page from the stack of letters in front of her. "Look what came today!"

Clara pulled out a chair and scooted out another for Phoebe. "Who's it from?"

"Hugh! He's left New York, and I've just had the most marvelous idea. We must hold a ball to celebrate."

"That would be wonderful. When?"

"What about the 2nd of November? It's a little late to be considered a proper homecoming. He will have been here close to a month already; however, we need ample time to prepare."

Clara toyed with her lower lip. "Do you think Mrs. Simmons will allow her family to come? It'll likely be the only chance Virginia and Megan have left to attend a ball this year."

"The last for her sons also, and they aren't growing any younger, especially Charles." Lavinia reached for her letter opener. "Mahala's not unkind, and they have to come out of mourning eventually. Ed's been dead for over a year." When Clara grew silent, her mother's eyes flew up from her envelope. "Oh, no. I know that look. I love Charles too, but your father simply won't consider him for you."

"But why? All through my childhood, Father treated him like a second son. Now that he's hired him as our foreman…" She glanced up sharply. "Is that it? Because Charles is now an employee?"

Phoebe began fiddling with the folds of her skirt, wishing she could sneak away.

"Clara, you know your father better than that. He has his reasons—very good ones.[i] Besides, there are practical considerations. Where would you live? With Charles caring for his mother and the younger children, their home is crowded as it is."

"We could live here."

Lavinia shook her head. "And who will work their farm?"

"Why can't William? He is only a few years younger."

"They are an important 'few years,' and he's never taken to farming. I hear he got a job in Mr. Yancy's store."

Clara slumped back against her wicker chair. "It's just not fair."

"I'm well acquainted with those feelings, Honey. Honestly, I am; but there isn't a thing either you or I can do about it. Your father is adamant."

"But…"

Lavinia lifted a well-manicured hand, signaling she would hear no more of it. "Speaking of the Simmonses, Phoebe, would you pay them a visit on your way home? We have too much to do today to start writing invitations, but I'd like them to know our plans as soon as possible. And here, take them this issue of Godey's. It arrived today, and after a year of mourning, I expect their gowns will need refreshing."

"Well." Clara smirked. "If father won't let Charles court me, I can at least peek at the latest competition. Phoebe says they have a young woman staying with them who is 'lonely and alone.'"

"Not us; the Nelsons."

"Oh, yes." Lavinia turned toward Phoebe. "You mentioned something earlier. Who is she?"

"A woman we found on our doorstep last night."

"A beggar?"

"I don't think so. Her shoes were worn thin, but both they and her garments were of high quality."

"Where did she come from?"

"We have no idea. She was still unconscious when the Nelsons took her home."

"Unconscious?" Clara's eyes grew wide.

Phoebe nodded. "She seems to have fainted while reaching for our door."

Lavinia gaped. "And you say she is with the Nelsons?"

"Mother." Clara curved her lips. "It has been far too long since we've called at River Bend—nearly an entire month."

"I'm intrigued, but how can we spare the time? The entire staff is scouring the house, and I was hoping that you and Phoebe would help me cut and arrange flowers. We will need three bouquets for the bedrooms alone."

"I'd be happy to," replied Phoebe.

"It's a shame that our lilacs are no longer blooming."

"Why three?" Clara cocked her head. "Is he bringing guests?"

"Two men we hope will invest in our whiskey production. One is some sort of royalty. Your father wants everything to be perfect."

# Chapter 3

WHEN RUBY PEEKED out the Simmonses' front door, she broke into a wide grin. "Good afternoon, Missy Farrell. Take a seat in the parlor while I fetch Missus Mahala."

"Ruby, wait." Phoebe whispered. "I have a message from your sister."

"Mitilde?"

"Yes. She said, 'Jubal is set to accompany the station master straight up the line before the month's end.'"

"My boy, Jubal? He gonna ride *the train*?" Ruby shook with joy until she peered into Phoebe's face. "What's the matter? Your eyes is as big as…you 'spect somethin' may go wrong?"

"No." Phoebe shook her head. "I only just now grasped what the message meant"

"You doesn't know 'bout…?" Ruby's mahogany features suddenly sobered. "You best be forgettin' *all* you thinks you be graspin.'"

"I will. Forget I said…" She paused, craning her neck to see whose footsteps she heard.

"Why, it's Phoebe Farrell." Mahala Simmons held out her ample hands in welcome, her wheat-colored hair pinned atop her head. "Whatever are you thinking, Ruby, keeping Miss Farrell standing by the door? Go and fetch us some lemonade. Girls, we have a visitor."

While Mrs. Simmons ushered Phoebe to the parlor, her ginger-headed daughter, Virginia, darted from her room. "Am I glad to see you!" Her green eyes echoed the greeting. "Sit down and give us the news. Charles and William never tell us anything."

Megan, more auburn-haired and almost two years younger, flounced down by Phoebe's other side. "Have you heard about the woman staying with the Nelsons?"

"Of course, she has, Meg." Mrs. Simmons sat across from them. "Mary told us Augie came up with her name."

Phoebe dimpled. "Did you meet her?"

"Yes, this morning when my girls and I called at River Bend. Mrs. Nelson hopes the bunch of you will ride over each Saturday to discuss an agreed upon book. I suggested Jane Austen's novels. You can't find a more welcoming woman than Mary, but you know how quiet Emily can be. Mary is afraid her patient may grow bored."

"What a wonderful idea. Then she is awake and recovering well?"

Megan's hazel green eyes turned soft with sympathy. "She looks so troubled, all sadness and confusion. She can barely remember a thing."

"Convenient, I'd say," countered Virginia. "I don't believe half of it. More likely, she's running from someone."

"From whom?" asked eleven-year-old Sarah. When she had spotted Phoebe driving up the lane, she had plunked down her milking pail in the straw and rushed through the back door.

Virginia shrugged. "Probably the law. Rather wily, if you ask me, to hide with a family everybody trusts and answer every question with 'I'm afraid I don't recall.'"

Megan gaped at her sister as if she had kicked a kitten. "She didn't choose the Nelsons; she chose the parsonage. Isn't that right, Phoebe?"

"Yes. She was unconscious when the Nelsons took her with them. Do you have a reason to suspect she's pretending?"

"No. I'm just not as trusting as Megan and you."

"Wouldn't we be kinder to take her word?"

Virginia slung her eyes sideways. "Kinder or just foolish? Jesus didn't trust everyone.[ii] Your pa said so in his sermon last Sunday."

Phoebe paused to accept the glass of lemonade Ruby handed her. "I don't think Papa was advising us to be cynical. It's true, Jesus didn't always divulge His thoughts; He *knew* which men He could or couldn't trust. They're not the same."

Little Sarah looked baffled. "Why not?"

"Guarding yourself against a known threat is different than accusing someone—even in your heart—without evidence."

"Pshaw! So, you believe everything any stranger tells you?"

"No, but…" Phoebe took a deep breath while she gathered her thoughts.

"Daughters, I believe Phoebe is trying to say, 'Love believes all things.'[iii] If this young woman were one of you, I'd hope folks would help her first and satisfy their curiosity later. Phoebe, would you like more lemonade?"

"No thank you, ma'am. I should be leaving for The Lilacs." She set down her empty glass. "The Kikers are hosting a ball later in the month to welcome Hugh home. Mrs. Kiker sent me to tell you before the invitations go out.

She wanted your family to have as much notice as possible."

"Can we go, Ma?" All three of Mahala's daughters sat forward on their seats. "Please?"

Mrs. Simmons rubbed a finger over her lips. "I don't see why not."

"Oh, Ma," moaned Virginia. "What shall we wear?"

"Whatever we find in our trunks. If we are diligent, we'll have time to refashion some of your old gowns."

"Oh, I almost forgot." Phoebe reached into her netted bag. "Mrs. Kiker sent her latest copy of Godey's in case you wanted to page through it."

"Lavinia is always so considerate. Please tell her thank you. Girls, we must ask William if the store has stocked any new ribbon. Phoebe, did we tell you he is working for Mr. Yancy now?"

"That explains why we so rarely see him."

"He's a good son—and a hard worker. Mr. Yancy is lucky to have him, and since Charles works all day at The Lilacs, we have planted fewer crops. Of course, Jeremiah has extra responsibilities and grows lonely for his brothers' company, but that makes us doubly glad he has Augie."

Phoebe rose from her seat. "Augie feels the same."

"Please tell Lavinia thank you for us, and that our family is happy to attend."

# Chapter 4

LAVINIA LIFTED AN envelope from a stack of mail and fanned herself. "Land's sakes, it's humid, even in the shade." Plucking out the letter, she unfolded the pages. "Why, it's another from Hugh. From Pennsylvania. Phoebe, go find Clara and bring her out here."

"Do you know where she might be?"

"Look in the parlor. She was retrieving a book from the library, but that room catches little breeze."

Slipping into the house and down the hall, Phoebe found Clara reading *Pride and Prejudice*, the book decided upon for the Nelsons' gathering that Saturday.

"Your mother wants you to come outside."

"Good." She snapped the book shut. "I deplore reading, though I had just reached a good part. Did you visit the young mystery woman at the Nelsons'?"

"No. I intend to drop by today once I'm finished here."

"You may be wasting your time. We called last evening, but she had grown too tired to receive visitors."

"Oh."

"Stop puckering your brow. Nothing is wrong with her that a good dose of rest won't fix, or so says Emily. You should have seen Em when I told her Hugh was coming home. I thought *she* might faint dead right on the spot."

"Emily is more durable than people assume. She is reserved, not fragile."

"Well…I will have to take your word for that."

When they stepped out onto the veranda, Lavinia waved Hugh's letter in the air. "He may be here tonight, Clara, or at latest tomorrow! And, Phoebe, you'll never guess who he's bringing home."

"Besides the investors?"

"Hilda Auger's grandson, Aaron!"

Phoebe's mouth dropped open. Although Lavinia occasionally dictated letters to Mr. Auger, and he had corresponded with her father once or twice about his grandmother's estate, she had neither seen nor heard from him since she left his home just prior to Christmas. "Why…"

"I think we all know *why*." Lavinia grinned. "That same lovely color flushes your cheeks each time I send him a letter."

Phoebe was glad when Mitilde bumped the door open to bring out a tray.

"Here's the coffee you was wantin' Missus Lavinia, an' I added one of my tastiest pastries for you, Missy Phoebe. You gots to keep sweet for when that beau of yers arrives."

"He's not my…wait, how did you know…does everybody…"

"Now Phoebe." Lavinia patted her hand. "Don't go turning yourself inside out. I promise to stop teasing you so unmercifully. Mitilde came out a minute ago so I could read her a letter from her niece. You remember Beatrice, don't you?"

"Yes." Phoebe cautiously flicked her eyes to Clara's, fighting hard to keep from dimpling at the name. "During the weeks I served as Mrs. Auger's companion, she worked in the kitchen. How is she?"

"She fine." Mitilde broke into a huge grin. "Gonna have a baby."

Phoebe lost the battle with her dimples, but it did not matter. Lavinia had captured Clara's attention.

"…I want you to take special care how you dress for dinner. As I mentioned the other day, one of Hugh's guests is titled, though he asked that we treat him as we would anyone. And I believe Hugh wrote both men are widowed. Let me find the correct paragraph." Lavinia scanned the letter. "Here it is. 'The losses of their wives seem to have drawn them together. I am hoping a change of venue will do each one good.'" Folding the pages, she peered over her spectacles at her daughter. "Why don't you wear your new indigo gown? It compliments your sapphire eyes."

"For two widowers? They are likely to be Father's age."

"Father's age or not, they will need comfort, so you must do your best to offer it. Who knows? Men with experience possess a certain charm, and it is high time you married. You will soon turn twenty-two, and we can all attest how few desirable suitors are in our circle."

Clara slumped in her chair, pushing out her lower lip. "It's just not fair. Hugh is bringing home an eligible and wealthy young man for Phoebe, and you relegate *me* to taking care of a couple old codgers."

# Chapter 5

WHILE PHOEBE WAS crossing the little stone bridge to the Nelson farm, she spied a mallard and her ducklings waddling up the riverbank. She had never seen a home more pleasantly situated. As she followed the winding pathway, she listened to the water rippling around the bend and felt herself relax. Indeed, everything about the Nelsons was soothing, from the colonel's kind manner to his wife Mary's gift for hospitality. Even her friend Emily added to the feeling. She radiated calm.

"We're over here!" called Mary, waving as Phoebe raised the brass lion's head to knock. She was sitting with Emily on one of two swings hanging from a shady arbor.

Phoebe could not tell who was rocking its twin, though the dressing gown and swath wrapping her hair were both familiar. As she drew closer, she supposed this might be the unexpected addition to her father's birthday dinner.

The woman rose and held out her hand. "I am afraid Mary and Emily cannot properly introduce us; I seem to have forgotten who I am. They tell me your brother christened me Isabela."

Phoebe dimpled. "He's at a fanciful stage."

"Please sit with me." Isabela patted the wide swing.

"Thank you. I am glad you are feeling better. You gave us quite a scare on Sunday. We, Augie and I, searched for your reticule to see if we could find something that might identify you."

"Did I have one?" Her green eyes tilted up at the outer edges, reminding Phoebe of a housecat. "All I can remember is the pain of my empty stomach and the fear I could no longer go on."

"I do not know, but we didn't find any. My family will be relieved to hear how well you appear."

"Yes, I am well. Perfectly. Mary has been looming over me like a mother bear."

Although Mrs. Nelson, or Mama Nelson as Augie and she had lately begun calling her, was appropriately protective of those within her sphere, Phoebe found it hard to picture her as a huge, lumbering beast. She exuded elegance that would befit President Tyler's new wife.

"And Emily has been keeping me…" Isabela paused, an odd expression wafting across her face.

"What is it?" asked Mary. "Are you feeling poorly?"

"I do not know." Isabela closed her eyes, pressing the back of her hand against her forehead before continuing. "Please excuse me. I am not myself. An odd sensation, a great sadness began hovering close, but it has moved away now beyond my grasp."

"With ample food and a good amount of rest, you will return to your old self in no time. Meanwhile, girls, shall we pray for her? Would that be alright, Isabela?"

"I would welcome your prayers."

After they had done so, Phoebe hopped off the swing. "Well, now that I've seen you are all right, I need to get home before I lose the light."

Isabela clasped her hand. "Thank you for checking on me. And please, tell your family how grateful I am."

"We did nothing but pass you to Colonel and Mrs. Nelson."

"Your family opened the door. I do not call that 'nothing'."

"I will be happy to convey the message. My parents will be pleased. I would be surprised if one or both did not call on you soon, though they will give you a few days to make certain you are well enough for visitors. I'll see you Saturday."

"I am eager to meet your friends. And your brother, should I hope to see him again?"

"He would be thrilled."

"What did you call him?"

"Augie—really August—and he is more likely to become a pest."

"Ah, the little brother. How I have missed mine."

WHEN PHOEBE ARRIVED home at the parsonage, Augie scrambled down so hastily from his treehouse, he missed the last rung and landed on his backside; but he jumped up and scampered toward her before she climbed from the wagon.

"Are you all right?"

"Yeah." He dusted dirt and grass from his britches. "Did you see her—the lady from Sunday evening?"

"I did, and guess what name she told me to call her?"

"What?"

"'Isabela.'"

Her brother broke into a pleased grin. "That's her real name?"

"No, she doesn't remember her own, but the Nelsons told her you called her that, and she seems to like it."

"What is she like?"

Before Phoebe could respond, their parents stepped out the front door and began peppering her with their own questions: "Is she up and about? What did she have to say?"

"I can't answer everyone at once." Phoebe laughed as she held up her hands. "She looked well enough and had lovely manners, very appreciative of the care the Nelsons are giving her. She asked me to convey her thanks for our part. Her main difficulty seems to be her memory: she can't say who she is."

"That's an odd effect from hunger," replied the reverend.

"Maybe she hit her head, Ernest, when she fell by our door."

Augie's eyes gleamed. "Or maybe she fell while escaping a *dungeon*."

His father flicked him an amused glance. "Amelia, we need to order Augie some more sensible literature, perhaps a history of Europe. I doubt there is a castle in the whole of the United States."

"Oh, Ernest, he is only nine and has a wonderfully vivid imagination."

"Well…" He ruffled his son's hair. "Let's go inside. We can quiz your sister while we are eating dinner."

AS PHOEBE WAS wiping a towel across the clean plate Amelia passed to her, she wondered why her mother's dimples, so like her own, kept twitching. She appeared to be fighting hard to hold back a smile.

"Well?" her mother asked. "Are you excited?"

"About what, Mama?"

"Mr. Auger, of course."

Phoebe stopped her drying. "How did you hear?"

"Your father received a note today. He thought you might prefer to be surprised, but I persuaded him otherwise. No young woman likes to be caught unprepared."

"For what?"

Amelia leaned in close. "He asked Papa for permission to call on you."

The plate Phoebe was drying slipped from her hand. "I'm sorry, Mama. Stay still while I get those shards by your feet."

"Are you two all right?" Her father rounded the doorframe. One glimpse of his daughter's face answered his question.

"Kitten, I wanted to tell you during dinner, but with Augie at the table. . . Your mama and I thought you would be pleased. He hasn't made any formal requests—just permission to call while he's here."

Phoebe swept up the remaining pieces and dumped them in a bin her mother took and set aside.

"We were impressed by the respect he showed your father by asking. Not all men would. Do you have feelings for someone else? Hugh, perhaps, or that man who works with Matthew Bentley?"

The color that had already been inflaming Phoebe's cheeks deepened. "I doubt I will ever see Mr. Dyer again,

Mama, and though I regard Hugh highly, you know what Emily's feelings are."

"Then what is it? Is there something about his person you dislike?"

"No, he is a fine man, but after embarrassing myself with Samuel, I've been determined not to…give my imagination any rein."

"That is precisely why your mother and I so valued his asking. Such conventions seem cumbersome to someone of your age, but they prevent misunderstandings. I haven't consented. He's presently en route. I will politely refuse him if you prefer."

"I do not know what I feel, but…" Phoebe hesitated, unsure how to put her thoughts into words.

"He is only paying you a call. It will offer you a chance to see if you still enjoy his company."

Phoebe picked at her fingernails. "It is just so sudden."

"You met each other half a year ago."

"Yes—*met*. That is all."

"He gave me the impression the two of you had become friends."

"We had the promising beginning of a friendship, but I have not heard from him since."

"That, Kitten, is further evidence of his integrity. A man should not correspond with a woman until he determines his intentions."

Amelia leaned over to kiss Phoebe's temple. "He is likely to be at the Kikers' when you arrive for work in the morning. You'd better get a good night's sleep."

# Chapter 6

PHOEBE LAID DOWN her pen once she heard masculine voices. During the ride up The Pike, her stomach had felt like a butter churn under a particularly vigorous hand. Clara had not helped. As soon as Phoebe had stepped across The Lilacs' threshold, the young woman's eyes had slowly climbed from her boot tips to her hair ribbon, a smile playing about her lips.

"Why, don't you look fetching this morning? Mother will be pleased. Oh, don't worry—none of them are up yet. Go hide in Mother's writing room, and we'll call you when they rise."

Clara had been right. As soon as Lavinia caught a glimpse of Phoebe, she stopped, stepped back, and inspected her at arm's length. "How nicely that mossy shade brings out the green around your eyes."

Phoebe hoped so. She had picked the frock for just that reason. Next to Clara's, her eyes held all the appeal of a sparrow beside a blue jay. Why she cared, she found it harder to work out. Her attraction to Mr. Auger had deepened during the days after his grandmother's death, but Mama had guessed the truth last night. Mr. Dyer's surprising ways had effectively eclipsed it. How, she could not explain. She had barely shared half a week with the young detective and maybe ten sentences.

Glancing out the writing room's window, Phoebe noticed the sun was climbing above the treetops. She could not blame the travelers for sleeping in. Kitch told her they had arrived well after supper and had stayed up late regaling the household with stories of their adventures. Whose adventures exactly, Phoebe began to wonder when a gentle knock drew her attention to the door.

"Good morning." When the younger Mr. Kiker slipped around it, smiling broadly, Phoebe jumped up and nearly flung her arms around him.

"Hugh! How are you? How was Europe? I was… everyone was…so happy to learn you were finally coming home."

"Hold on." His dark eyes snapped with humor. "I brought you something." Reaching into his pocket, he drew out a small box and straightened the ribbon. "I picked it up in the south of France."

"For me?" When Phoebe lifted the lid, she found an oval with a small painted bird, reminding her of their first meeting. "It's beautiful, but I can't…"

"Of course, you can. I bought a similar one for Emily, only hers is a horse. Here, let me pin it on."

As he lifted the brooch from the box, raising her chin with his finger and settling the piece over her top button, she took in the thick lashes she remembered so well and the dark hair curling around his ears and collar.

He stepped back to assess how it looked. "Lovely."

Though his drawl was rich and deep, his expression was so like his mother's earlier, she could not help but dimple. She touched the piece's cool, smooth surface. "Thank you. I'm sure to wear it often."

Clara swung back the door and leaned into the room. "What have we here? If Mr. Auger catches you gazing at my brother like that, he may challenge him to a duel."

"Phoebe!" They heard Lavinia calling from the hall. "I'm heading out to the veranda. Come join me. Have you seen my children? Mitilde has fixed us all brunch."

While Clara swirled after her mother, Hugh held the door to let Phoebe pass through to the foyer. Once she crossed it and stepped outside, she met a pair of warm eyes, a shade or two lighter than Hugh's nearly black ones. "Miss Farrell." Aaron Auger pulled out the wicker chair next to his. "It's a pleasure to see you again."

"You also, Mr. Auger." She took the seat.

Clara swiveled toward the outbuilding that held The Lilacs' office. "Mother, where are Daddy and Hugh's other two friends?"

"Asa went to the brewery, Honey, and the Englishmen are still sleeping."

Mr. Auger pushed in Phoebe's chair and sat down. "I've never travelled to Europe, but I've heard it is hard to adjust to the change in time."

"I don't know why." Clara flounced down into a chair beside her mother. "They had nothing to do on the ship but sleep, and it's not like they only arrived. They've been in the country for nearly a week."

Hugh squeezed his sister's hand. "Traveling is more tiresome than you might think it. Besides, I'm delighted to see my favorite girls while I have fewer competitors for their attention." He glanced from her to his mother to Phoebe.

"You'd better not let Emily hear you talking like that," Clara teased.

"Who is Emily?" asked Mr. Auger.

"The granddaughter of old family friends," Hugh answered.

"Don't be so modest," continued Clara. "She has moped around after him since she was in pigtails."

"You mean she doesn't still wear them?"

"Now children," interrupted their mother, "you mustn't fill Mr. Auger's head with silly notions. Emily is a lovely young woman from a fine family. True, she once favored Hugh, but many girls outgrow their childhood affections." She slid her eyes toward her son. "Who knows? Maybe she and Mr. Whitcomb will take a shine to each other."

"Who is Mr. Whitcomb?" asked Phoebe.

"One of Hugh's English guests."

"Ugh!" Clara scrunched up her nose. "How could you wish him on poor Emily? I found him downright bothersome last evening. He lectured me about the naivete of young women who become attached too easily to a handsome face or fortune. I do believe he was warning me off, as if I would ever fancy him. He even implied I should be wary of you, Mr. Auger."

"Me? Why?"

"I simply cannot imagine. I believe his words were, 'Take your brother's friend as an example,' but Father interrupted, inviting him to inspect the brewery this morning."

Aaron adjusted his position and tossed Phoebe an uncertain glance. "I just met the man."

"Oh, Honey, don't give it another thought." Lavinia fluttered her hand dismissively. "And Clara, do try to be kind. Some men are deeply affected by the loss of their wives. Although he does seem a bit…glum, I admire the depth he must have felt for her." She slid her eyes toward her son and offered him a wily smile. "Emily might be the perfect tonic for…"

"Mother." Hugh chuckled. "Have you taken up match-making in my absence?"

"Not at all." She unfurled her napkin as the cook brought out flapjacks. "Thank you, Mitilde. I am simply warning you not to take Emily's admiration for granted. One day, you may wake up and see what a charming young woman she has become."

Clara pulled in her chin. "Emily? Thoughtful, yes. I'll even grant you very pretty, but I would hardly say charming."

"Many men find an understanding heart the most entrancing of all qualities. Wouldn't you say so, Aaron?"

Mr. Auger slid his eyes toward Phoebe. "I would, especially when combined with a fine mind and lovely eyes."

Mitilde, to Phoebe's relief, chose that moment to lean between them with a platter filled with bacon and sausage. Why, she wondered, did she feel so tongue-tied? She had eaten breakfast beside this man every morning during the past yuletide. "How is your little brother?"

"Wil's coming into his own now that his mother and Patrick are married. Quite the little man."

"Wil?"

Aaron nodded. "Says it sounds more grown up. He made me promise to bring this to you." He reached down beside his chair and lifted a well-worn lop-eared stuffed rabbit onto her lap.

"Captain Cuddlebunny?"

"He told me he's outgrown him, but he wishes him to be safe and well-loved."

"Safe?"

"I suspect his stepfather thinks he is too old for such toys. Wil feared he might one day find him missing."

Phoebe gasped, embracing the bunny as if he were Aaron's brother. As she stroked his long ears, his head tilted back, offering the illusion he was returning her gaze.

"I assure you he rode in style, his head peeking out of my bag so he could catch the scenery."

"How kind of you. Please tell your brother I will cherish him."

"Look, Hugh!" Lavinia waved to their foreman as he crossed the stable yard. "There's Charles! I'm not sure he's heard you're back." Rising off her chair, she waved again. "Charles! Come, join us for brunch."

The man removed his hat, leaping two steps at a time until he reached the veranda and halted in surprise. "When did you get home?" Grabbing Hugh by the hand, he pulled him close and slapped him soundly on the back. "I took you for Asa."

"Great to see you, old man! Father's in the brewery."

"Europe must have agreed with you. You look good."

"So do you. I wish you could've come. Let me introduce you to our guest. Aaron, this is Charles Simmons, my brother of sorts and The Lilacs' foreman. Charles, this is Aaron Auger. Bring over another chair. Clara won't mind scooting over for you."

While Hugh winked at his sister, Charles stretched his neck toward the stable. "I wondered whose mounts I spotted this morning. Fine horses, but I counted four."

"They're Mr. Auger's. We—a couple of acquaintances from England and I—stayed the night with him in Pennsylvania, and since he had an errand here, we rode down together."

While Charles was taking his seat, Clara leaned close to him and smiled. "Mother has been trying to convince me that men prefer docile women."

"I never said docile, dear," Lavinia corrected. "Sweet tempered."

"Well?" Clara nudged his arm. "What do *you* think?"

The foreman began twisting the brim of his hat. "I don't like to contradict your mother, but I prefer a woman with a little fire, one whom—if need be—will put me in my place."

Aaron glanced from him to Hugh. From the darkness of their hair to the set of their chins, the likeness between them was remarkable, except for their eyes. Charles's were as strikingly blue as the other members of Hugh's family. "Did you say you are brothers?"

"'*Of a sort*'," Lavinia interjected. "Charles's late father was our previous foreman, so the boys were together so frequently, I imagine even my daughter regards him as a brother."

Clara mumbled an unintelligible retort, but the look she threw Charles declared everything she dared not say. As her lip jutted out, Phoebe felt such a sharp twinge of sympathy, she almost felt startled. Clara had not been easy to like.

Aaron took a sip of Mitilde's strongly brewed coffee. "Miss Farrell, if you haven't any objection, I would like to escort you home after you have finished work for the day. Your father and I have a few matters to discuss."

While dropping her eyes, Phoebe willed the rising heat to stay below her neckline.

"You needn't worry about propriety," Lavinia assured her. "Aaron will ride one of his horses, so no one need bring him back afterward."

"My parents will be pleased to make your acquaintance. Naturally, I told them about the weeks I spent with your grandmother. I only wish they could also meet William."

Charles cocked his head in her direction. "I know you can't mean my brother. They've known him since last spring."

"Not yours, Mr. Auger's. The owner of this little bunny."

"While visiting us before Christmas," explained Aaron, "Miss Farrell and my young step-brother grew deeply attached."

Clara leaned so close to the foreman, her shoulder pressed against his shirt. "It would appear, Charles," she drawled, "we have uncovered an Auger family trait."

# Chapter 7

ONCE OUTSIDE THE Lilacs' gate, Mr. Auger pulled his mount beside the parsonage wagon. "I am enjoying your valley, Miss Farrell. The rolling hills are not so different than Allentown, but we lack your view of the mountains."

"This time of day is my favorite." She nodded toward the east. "I love the golden light the sun casts across the Blue Ridge as it sets."

"They appear to be glowing. Would you be grieved to leave the area? I remember how homesick you grew while staying with us."

"I did, but Christmas is a special time, and our families are what we miss most while away, don't you think?"

"Indeed, though some families are not as close as yours. I look forward to meeting them. Has your father mentioned my most recent letter?"

"Yes." Phoebe's mouth went dry. "He told me he received one the day before yesterday." She forced herself to smile up at him, though her mind felt like boiling water, all chaos and confusion. When a train of several wagons carrying goods to New Market approached from the opposite direction, she was glad they compelled him to drop behind her if only a short while.

"I've often pondered our conversations and have been reading Grandmother's Bible. I hope to discuss questions I have with your father."

Phoebe's shoulders relaxed. "He would enjoy answering them. Would you mind if I listened?"

"I'd hoped you would want to. It's only fitting since you played an important part in stirring them. However, I have another matter to discuss with him that will require us to speak privately, so if you do not mind…"

He inclined his head, searching her face. It was all she could do not to look away.

"Not at all. I hope the two of you will become friends."

***

AUGIE AND SPARKLES came springing up to Phoebe once she and Mr. Auger parted: he toward the church study and she up the path to the parsonage.

"Where'd you get the rabbit?" He snatched the cloth bunny out of Phoebe's hand, holding it aloft above Sparkles.

"Give that back!" The retriever darted away as Phoebe lunged after it.

"Why the big fuss? It's all tattered."

"He is not an 'it.' His name is Captain Fluffy Cuddlebunny. He's a…*gift* from Mrs. Auger's little grandson and very precious."

Augie shrugged. "Did you see Isabela?"

"Not today. A friend of…Hugh's…escorted me home."

"Hugh? He's back from Europe?"

"Yes. I am sorry; I meant to tell you yesterday. He returned last evening and brought several guests with him."

"From Europe? Like Hessians?"

Phoebe peered at him skeptically. "Why would you guess that?"

"'Cause of the story Colonel Nelson was telling us. You know—about the prisoners who walked the ridge to buy his grandmother's apple pies."

"That was half a century ago, during the War of Independence. Hugh's visitors are from London."

"Why would they want to come here?"

"Ask Mr. Auger. He is with Papa."

"Why?" An interest in his sister clearly never crossed his mind.

"Um… He didn't…"

"Wait a minute." Augie's hazy blue eyes started to twinkle. "Isn't he the man you were visiting before Christmas? The one who writes to Papa?"

"I wasn't 'visiting' him. His grandmother hired me as a companion."

"Then why are you turning all red?"

"I'm not…"

"Are too! Phoebe's got a caller…"

"Don't you dare, Augie. I suspect Papa will invite him to dinner, so be on your best behavior."

When a door opened in front of them, their mother walked out. "There you are, Phoebe. What a sweet little bunny. Come help me set the table. Allison Wilson dropped by earlier and told us to expect company."

"How did she know?"

"John and Asa had some sort of meeting at The Lilacs. Something about this year's rye. I'm surprised you didn't see him."

“He may have gone straight to Mr. Kiker’s office.” They ducked back into the parsonage. “Why did Aunt Allison come by?”

“She was on her way to the Nelsons’. Mary asked her to lend them all her Austen books so that Emily and ‘Isabela’ might have their own copies. That poor woman. Imagine waking up in a strange home with people you had never seen much less known.”

“I would be scared out of my wits.”

“I saw your Mr. Auger riding with you up the lane. I hope he brought his appetite. I’ve roasted a beef brisket and am making peach cobbler. It’s so much simpler than baking a pie.”

***

PHOEBE WAS PLACING the cobbler in the oven when she heard her father’s voice from the dining room.

“Mr. Auger, this is Mrs. Farrell, my wife, and our son, August—Augie for short. Amelia, where is Phoebe?” The reverend craned his neck in every direction.

“I’m here, Papa.” She hurried through the back door. “The stove needed more kindling.”

“Well, let’s all sit down. Amelia, the meal looks delicious.”

Taking his place at the head of the table, Reverend Farrell said the blessing, asked their guest for his plate, and loaded it up with the best portion of the roast. “Here you go. Augie, please pass Mr. Auger the mashed potatoes.”

While Aaron complimented her mother on each dish, Phoebe wandered through her memories of the Augers’ huge kitchen. It was inside the home, in the lowest floor, not attached to the back as the Farrells' was. There, 'Cook' was never called by her name, and the tasks Phoebe was performing were relegated to Beatrice, her helper. When Aaron smiled up to her as she served him dessert, she wondered if any of the same thoughts had been crossing his mind.

***

REVEREND AND MRS. Farrell bid their guest farewell, signaling Augie to take Sparkles for his late evening walk.

"Well, Ernest, what were you and Aaron talking about for so long before coming to supper? I half-assumed you'd refused him."

Phoebe looked from one to the other.

"No. He has my approval. We spoke at length about the path he was taking. It would make no sense at all for our Phoebe to be walking down one avenue while he headed up another."

"What did he respond?"

"He gave me plentiful reasons to rejoice over the young woman our daughter has become." Reverend Farrell slipped his arm around Phoebe's shoulder. "She stirred his thoughts about his purpose for existing."

"It was a natural thing to discuss, Papa, considering the passing of his grandmother."

"Well, Ernest, what did he *say*?"

"Once he began delving into the Scriptures, he became aware of a disparity between Jesus' words and his opinion of himself. The progression he described brought The Beatitudes to mind."

"What do you mean, Papa?"

"A man must first mourn his own lack, Kitten, before he can hunger and thirst for righteousness. Now that you have seen him again, do you wish to know him better?"

Phoebe dropped her gaze to the plank floor, recalling the care Aaron took with his brother's toy. He surely endured a good deal of ribbing from his companions. "Yes, Papa. I think I do."

# Chapter 8

ONCE PHOEBE ARRIVED at The Lilacs the next morning, she found the Kikers, Aaron Auger, and Charles Simmons drinking coffee on the Veranda. Clara was pouring tea for their two English guests, eliciting both her mother's smile and Charles's frown.

All six men stood up once Phoebe climbed the steps.

"Mr. Pinder and Mr. Whitcomb," began Asa Kiker, "please allow me to present Phoebe Farrell. She started as my wife's secretary but has become more a member of our family. Aaron, I understand you are already acquainted."

While Aaron nodded and the Englishmen bowed, Phoebe tried to sort out which name belonged to which man. She had been making certain her skirts cleared the porch, lest she trip and fall into them, and Mr. Kiker's acknowledgements had been brief.

Aaron grabbed a chair from the other end of the porch while Mitilde brought her a coffee cup. "Miss Farrell, please sit by me."

"Thank you."

As Clara occupied the two Englishmen, Phoebe had a chance to observe them. Both were well dressed and suitably groomed, but beyond that, they were like morning and evening. The fairer of the two was handsome in an entirely different way from Hugh or Aaron, though she guessed he was about their age. His features were regular and fine, almost pretty, and his expression was mild and sunny. She supposed the darker man to be nearly a decade older. His deeply set eyes were tucked beneath a prominent forehead, and his nose and chin were strong and angular.

Underscoring these differences was their disparity of demeanor. The younger was gentle and his voice so soft she strained to hear him. The elder's answers were terse, and he sounded gruff and gravelly.

After taking a sip of her coffee, Phoebe leaned closer to Aaron. "Do you know the Kikers' English guests well?"

"No, I met them on the eve of our journey here. Hugh wired me from New York requesting lodgings for the night."

Clara laughed at something too low to hear and then clapped with delight. "Oh, gentlemen, I almost forgot to tell you. We are holding a ball in honor of my brother's homecoming. I *do* hope you will be able to attend."

Her fair companion looked inclined to grant her anything she asked. "When will it be?"

"The first Saturday in November." She cast him a coquettish glance. "*Please* say you will."

The darker man scowled. "I'm sorry, Miss Kiker. You will have to excuse us. In a fortnight, we are expected in Williamsburg."

"Two weeks? Can't you postpone?" Clara turned her sweetest pout on the fairer Englishman, who in turn addressed Lavinia.

"Is the date for your ball already fixed?"

"I suppose not." She slanted a finger across her lips. "We haven't yet written out the invitations, but the earliest we could pull it off is October 26th. We will need to arrange for musicians and bring in any food items we do not raise." Lavinia paused. "Now that you suggest it, the end of the month will be better traveling for families like Phoebe's who don't own carriages. The moon will be full."

"Mother, that's hardly enough time for a new gown."

"It will have to be if you wish to dance with our guests."

Clara slid the younger Englishman a winning smile. "If Mr. Pinder can alter his schedule, I'm sure I can make do."

"Well, Whitcomb. You have heard our hostesses. Since they are willing to accommodate us, we can surely accommodate them. How could I deny Miss Kiker such a small pleasure?"

"It isn't decent." Mr. Whitcomb tossed his napkin onto the table. "We are both still in mourning."

"Nonsense!" As Mr. Pinder jerked up his fair head, Phoebe caught her first clear glimpse into his eyes. They were the color of forget-me-nots and held an innocent, almost childlike, surprise. "In several circles of my acquaintance, the standard period for a gentleman is three months. Genevieve has been… gone… a great deal longer."

"Wonderful!" Clara beamed. "Hugh, will you take me to Winchester? The dressmaker there is quicker than Strasburg's."

"Would you permit me to accompany you, also?" asked Mr. Pinder. "I am eager to see a frontier town."

The glance Hugh flicked Phoebe was rife with humor. "Then you will be disappointed. The frontier is over those mountains." He swiveled his head west.

"Phoebe." Aaron nudged her arm. "What was that look about?"

"You weren't supposed to see it." She dimpled. "At my first Lilac Ball, I implied the valley was filled with rubes."

Hugh leaned in and smiled. "She was surprised we found fiddlers who played Mozart and that I managed to stay off her toes."

Phoebe's cheeks flamed. "I wish he was exaggerating."

"Mother," said Clara, "you've already drawn up your list. While the bunch of us go to town, Phoebe can stay to pen the invitations. If anyone is to come, we must get them out at once." She fluttered her eyelashes toward Charles, who had grown uncharacteristically silent.

"I beg you to excuse me, Miss Kiker," answered the older Englishman, his mouth drooping as deeply as Charles's.

"Why, of course, Mr. Whitcomb. But from which, our outing or the ball?"

The man twisted his lips so disdainfully Phoebe expected he would decline both. "Your outing. Since Pinder has set aside his mourning for your ball; I would lack grace were I to refuse."

"Well, that settles it," declared Lavinia. "We are delighted. "Charles, your mother has already accepted for your family. I hope you will come too."

The foreman cast his clear blue eyes from Clara to Pinder, who was laughing at some comment she had whispered. "I will be there. You have my word."

***

"OH DEAR, PHOEBE." Lavinia fanned herself with the sample invitation she had composed. "I fear I have bitten off more than I can chew. Year after year, we throw our

Lilac Ball, but to offer these Englishmen a proper taste of American hospitality, I am afraid we must increase my list to include friends in Richmond. Why did Clara have to mention it? And of course, it means enduring Mr. Whitcomb that much longer. He *is* so unpleasant."

She looked down at Phoebe who sat poised to write. "I suppose it is very unchristian of me to talk so of him. He *is* a guest in our house and by all accounts has good reason to be miserable. Only, you would think from his high-handed responses, he was England's crown prince. He has been here less than two days, and I am already wishing I could dump him out an upstairs window." She stopped abruptly and tilted her head. "You don't think he is do you—the crown prince? I once read about one masquerading as a commoner, tired of the constraints of royalty and all." She glanced at Phoebe again. "You are laughing at me."

"Only because I understand your feelings, though England's crown prince is about three. The Spectator carried his birth announcement while we were living in Princeton."

"Of course. The idea was ridiculous."

"I can work late today and, if necessary, bring invitations home to finish this evening."

"You are a dear, and I may need to take you up on it. Clara is right. We need to get them posted as soon as we can."

"She is clearly enjoying Mr. Pinder's company."

"Yes." Lavinia smiled. "And he hers. I would hate to part with her, but they would make an excellent match."

# Chapter 9

THE FOLLOWING AFTERNOON, Lavinia glanced at her timepiece. "My, my! It's after three. I am so glad we are nearly finished. Be a dear, Phoebe, and run upstairs to get my spectacles. I believe they are on the little table next to my side of the bed."

"Of course." Phoebe set down her steel pen, swished out into the hall, and turning the corner toward the stairs, gathered up her skirts. Once she reached the upper landing, she stopped, retracing her memories of the second story's layout. During her year as Lavinia's secretary, her duties had taken her upstairs only once, and she did not wish to intrude into someone else's quarters.

As she was laying her thumb to a cool, brass latch, she hesitated. Someone in an adjacent room was pulling open a series of drawers and sliding them shut again. She gathered Sari, The Lilacs' houseslave, must be returning one of the travelers' freshly laundered shirts to his chest. Hugh, Aaron, and Mr. Pinder were visiting a horse farm near Strasburg, and she had seen Mr. Whitcomb heading down the lane to the plantation office. Slipping into Asa and Lavinia's blue and gold bedroom, she quickly located the spectacles on a mahogany end table and was pulling the door closed when someone plowed into her.

A pair of large hands grasped her arms, bringing her face to face with the ill-tempered Englishman. "I beg your pardon. It's Miss Farrell, yes?"

Phoebe nodded while a paper fluttered to the carpet.

"I trust you are not injured?"

"I'm fine, sir. Just surprised." She examined Lavinia's rims to make certain they had not bent.

"Foolish of me to be reading while walking."

As he let her go and stepped toward the landing, Phoebe snatched up the sheet of paper: a bill of sale from a wigmaker in Baltimore. "Mr. Whitcomb, I believe this is yours."

Spinning on his heel, he snatched it from her hand, mumbling the briefest thanks as he turned around.

"Uhm…you are welcome." She listened to his footsteps rushing down the stairs and waited until they slowed near the bottom before venturing down herself.

***

MITILDE'S HUSBAND LOADED four boxes full of invitations into the wagon. "You sure, Missy Phoebe, you don't want me to 'company you?"

"Thank you, Kitch, but I'll be fine. They aren't heavy, and this way I can drive straight home. We have dinner plans tonight."

"If you's sure, Missy."

"I am." While Phoebe was scrambling onto the buckboard, something about his response niggled her. Perhaps it was the look that had flitted through his eyes. Although she minutely reviewed their conversation, she found nothing she said that might have given offense, until she stumbled over one word: plans. She took for granted the prerogative to make them. How must he feel to be deprived of it? She had the merest hint. While she was a child, her parents made plans and she simply complied. Still, whenever she had raised an objection, they heard her out. Kitch had no such option.

How much, she wondered while she traveled up The Pike, did Kitch know about Lavinia's efforts to conduct her staff to freedom? Mitilde knew; she was certain. Both her open mention of her niece's letter and the message she sent to Ruby confirmed it. Still, many wives kept secrets from their husbands. Lavinia, for one; though how she achieved it was a mystery. Phoebe had been present while Asa asked why they appeared to be unable to hold onto their house slaves. Surely, he did not imagine any had preferred to return to the fields. It was backbreaking, and by all accounts, his former manager had not been lenient. She surmised Asa might have asked the question for her benefit to hide his complicity.

Once Phoebe had arrived in Strasburg, she tied Esmeralda to the hitching post and lifted a box of invitations out of the wagon. While she struggled to load a second box onto the first, the fairer of the Kikers' guests appeared by her side.

"May I help you, Miss Farrell?" He tipped his fawn-colored top hat. She had never seen one of such a light hue, but it suited his soft blue eyes far better than the more common black silk. "Thank you, Mr. Pinder. Where are your companions?"

"Still at their friend's horse farm, I imagine, examining his most recent acquisitions—Narragansett Pacers, I believe. So, since I don't intend to buy any horseflesh, I availed myself of a chance to explore this quaint-looking town."

He took the second box from her hand and scooped up the remaining two. "Invitations, I take it, for the ball?"

"Yes. We've been working on them steadily since yesterday morning. I'm afraid I've worn a callous on my finger."

"Do you enjoy being in the Kikers' employ?"

"Oh yes. I worked briefly for a woman up north, but her family continually made me aware of my place."

"Not your country's way, eh? I quite admire America's egalitarian spirit."

"Is England very different?"

Mr. Pinder nodded. "Society is stratified, often ridiculously so. Take Mr. Auger. His family is in trade. If I were at home, my peers would discourage an association with him regardless of his wealth."

"And you think this is unfair?"

"Undoubtedly, though I cannot pretend I would encourage one of my sisters to marry him. He is an affable man, but she would find herself passed over by persons she now considers intimates. It is the unalterable way of things."

Had his eyes not held such remarkable innocence, she might have thought his regard for Aaron insincere. "I see. Do they share your feelings?"

"The eldest, absolutely. She is the practical sort. The younger is less acquainted with life and might, were she ardently attached, disregard sense."

Their discussion halted as they lifted the boxes to the counter, and Mr. Pinder bid her farewell. As she watched him through the large plate window, she felt grateful she lived in America. His words, though, stayed with her while she slipped across the street to Yancy's General Merchandise.

Virginia and Megan Simmons' flaxen-haired brother turned around behind the counter when he heard the bell jingle. "Good afternoon, Phoebe! May I help you with anything?"

"It's so nice to see you, William. Your mother said you were working here." She pulled out a small snippet of material from the gown Clara had given to her. "Would you happen to have any ribbon to match this?" Although she loved the salmon-pink color, she was aware yellows were more in fashion this year.

"Let me see."

As he pulled a drawer open, Phoebe removed the lid from the rock candy, picked up a piece with the tongs, and dropped it into a small paper cornucopia.

"How much do you need?"

"A yard? Enough for my hair and to fasten a pendant about my neck."

"Will this ribbon do? It's the same shade but a bit deeper."

"It's perfect. I don't need it wrapped. And please add this for Augie."

William weighed the candy on a small scale and told her the price for both.

"Will I see you at Hugh's homecoming ball?"

"Yes. I suspect the whole county will be there, and my sisters can talk of nothing else. Megan dreams of dancing with one of Hugh's English friends, though she will have our brother Charles breathing down her neck. He does not like him."

As Phoebe dug for coins, she did not ask which man he meant. It had to be Mr. Pinder. Clara appeared to be using him to egg Charles into pursuing her more aggressively, but if her mother's wishes were any indication, she might flirt herself onto a ship across the Atlantic.

"Frankly," continued William, "I am apt to agree with him."

"Oh?" She had observed several things about Mr. Pinder but none that were disagreeable.

"He has come in twice, asking if I have seen a certain woman."

Phoebe's head shot up. "A woman? Who?"

William shook his head. "I have no idea. I know no one that fits the description: raven-haired, lavish spender."

"Odd indeed. What is she to him, and why would he think she's here?"

"I can't answer either. He asked me to watch for her, pressed a sovereign into my palm, and walked out." William handed her the cornucopia and ribbon.

"A whole sovereign? He must be desperate to find her." She stashed her goods in her mesh bag. "I'll see you on the 26th, if not sooner."

She had expected to ponder one of The Lilacs' guests on her ride home, but she had not expected it to be Mr. Pinder.

# Chapter 10

ON SATURDAY, PHOEBE hopped down from the church wagon to open a pair of low wrought iron gates with an R for River and a B for Bend captured in their scrollwork. Since the Simmonses had told her Mary Nelson's plan, she had been eager for this day to arrive. *Pride and Prejudice*, the book they had decided to read first, rivaled *Persuasion* and *Northanger Abbey* for her favorite Austen. Judging by the fullness of the stable yard, she feared she was late and hurried up the path.

When she spotted a curricle, a smile curved her lips. It belonged to Allison and John Wilson whose married daughter, Lisa White, borrowed it on occasion. Phoebe hoped this was one of them, and as she crossed the home's threshold, her dimples deepened. Silhouetted by the entry hall's Palladian window was the young mother's statuesque form.

"Lisa, it is so nice to see you. I was wishing for you to come."

"I wouldn't miss it." The gathers about her empire waistline poorly concealed her anticipated second child.

"Look at you—your day is getting closer—and look at Jack!" The toddler glanced up from the small, carved horse he rocked back and forth imitating a quick gallop across the wooden floor. "He's grown so tall since I last saw him.

When we moved here last spring, he seemed a mature baby. Now he is a tiny man."

Lisa glowed. "I suspect he takes after my father. Jack's half a head taller than my friends' sons of his age."

Lisa's mother slipped up beside them, her dark eyes full of their usual sparkle, and gave Phoebe a brief hug. "I'll take Jack outside once Emily starts the discussion. You are looking well."

"You are, too, Auntie Allison. Had I known you would be here, I would have asked Mama and Lucy to come."

"We made the decision at the last minute. I intended to keep Jack with me, but…" She peered down at the folds over her daughter's midsection. "Lisa felt more comfortable having me close at hand, just in case."

"Ladies," called Mary Nelson. "If you will serve yourself, we are ready to begin." She inclined her head toward a table topped with tiers of miniature sandwiches and cakes. Stacks of cups and saucers perched beside them.

Once the young women moved to the parlor, Emily opened her book. "Has anyone read *Pride and Prejudice*?" She spoke so well, even Phoebe could not tell if she felt nervous, but when every head nodded, the glance she tossed her grandmother's retreating form belied her calm.

Isabela came to her rescue. "Then do you think it might be agreeable, Emily, to forgo the reading and head straight into our discussion?"

"What an excellent suggestion. Phoebe, you are smiling down at your book. Have you found something of interest?"

"It fell open to Jane Bennet's description of Mr. Bingley—the second paragraph of chapter four. 'He is just what a young man ought to be…sensible, good humored, lively; and I never saw such happy manners!—so much ease, with such perfect good breeding!'[iv] It bears a striking similarity to an Englishman who is staying with the Kikers. Don't you think so, Clara?"

"I do indeed, and…" she dropped her sapphire eyes to Elizabeth Bennet's answer. "'He is also handsome, which a man ought likewise to be, if he possibly can. His character is thereby complete.'[v]"

"Then," quipped Megan, pulling her shiny auburn curls to one shoulder, "we must find him a Jane, though Lisa personifies her so perfectly, I cannot imagine any other."

Phoebe glanced back at Clara, whom no one would confuse with Jane, but her mind seemed elsewhere.

Emily's was not. She heartily agreed with Megan and launched into the traits Jane and Lisa shared.

When others joined in, Lisa laughed and shook her head. "Stop, you are embarrassing me. Anyway, I already have my Mr. Bingley. I think his description sounds precisely like Jordan."

"Ah." Isabela purred from her place on a couch. "Your Jordan must be a fine man to earn praise from his own wife. I do not believe I have ever met such a man."

"Perhaps you will at our ball," offered Clara. "Besides the man Phoebe mentioned, we have two other guests, though they are not as promising. One is taken and the other perfectly fits Lizzy's first impressions of Darcy."

"Her *first*?" moaned Megan's older sister, Virginia. "He must be ghastly. Do you think, like Darcy, he might improve with time?"

Clara twisted a dark curl and shrugged. "Who can say? Lizzy describes everything I know of him." She thumbed back a few pages. "'He was discovered to be proud, to be above his company, and above being pleased.'"

Virginia fastened her eyes on Phoebe. "You'd best be careful, Clara. Our pastor's daughter may scold you for gossiping."

As each friend turned, a flush bloomed over Phoebe's cheeks.

"Ginny!" Megan scolded. "She did no such thing. She was encouraging you to stop being so suspicious of…" She stopped, suddenly aware she could say no more without deeply embarrassing their guest of honor.

Emily sat up straighter. "I have always appreciated Phoebe's mindfulness. She reminds me of Fanny Price, the protagonist in Mansfield Park. I would love to have Miss Price for a friend, but I am jumping into a later novel."

While she was speaking, Phoebe's eyes prickled. She knew what defending her cost Emily and could not imagine a truer friend.

"Ah, Phoebe," responded Isabela, "you inspire loyalty of a most precious kind. You are every bit as fortunate as Lisa. There are many kinds of love, no? A friend's loyalty is something to treasure."

Phoebe heartily agreed and felt grateful, also, to Isabela. She had deftly redirected the conversation, saving both her and Emily from needing to make further comment.

"And Mr. Wickham," continued Emily. "What do you think of him?"

"He was so amiable and gentlemanly," answered Megan, "that I hoped he might marry Lizzy, but then to discover his true nature…I was so disappointed."

Lisa nodded. "I would infer from the book's title, that was Miss Austen's point. Time and closer acquaintance rid us of our prejudices, whether they are in a person's favor or against him."

Isabela grew so quiet her very stillness drew everyone's attention. Glancing up, she seemed startled to meet all their gazes. "The most charming man I have ever known was also the cruelest."

As Phoebe strained to catch Isabela's words, her eyes and Virginia's collided, and she knew at once what the older girl was thinking. Worse, she could not argue, however much she would have liked to do so, and wondered when Emily spoke up, if she was purposefully changing the subject.

"I found the marriage of Charlotte Lucas and Mr. Collins interesting. Though Austen presents him as a fool, by accepting his imperfections, Charlotte appears to find a measure of happiness with him."

"Pshaw." Virginia pinned her with an incredulous stare. "Happiness or stretched patience? I couldn't tolerate a man who is so…groveling."

"I've discovered," offered Lisa, "the secret to a happy marriage is forgiveness. If you all knew me as Jordan now does, you would no longer think I am like Jane. I mean, it's easy to be like that man in the parable who demands repayment of a small debt. Jesus forgave me much; how can I hold Jordan's sins against him?"

Isabela put on a bright smile. "I hope each one of you finds your own Jordan, or Darcy, or Knightly, but much better to marry a kind-hearted buffoon like Mr. Collins than a rapscallion like Mr. Wickham."

"Have you been married, Isabela?" asked Virginia.

"But of course, my friend—to all the men I've met in these pages."

# Chapter 11

AMELIA FARRELL LAY a freshly baked loaf of bread on the table and then popped her head into the parlor. "Dinner is ready."

Augie jumped up from the bench and surveyed the table. "Chicken and gravy! Um-um."

"Everything smells delicious, Mama," added Phoebe. "I'm sorry I was not here to help you."

"I managed just fine. A chicken is not difficult to roast."

Ernest Farrell pulled in his chair and bowed his head. "Lord, we are sincerely thankful for the food you have provided and for a wife and mother who is an excellent cook."

"I'll say!" Augie beamed brightly at the plate his mother set before him. "Papa, please pass me the gravy."

"Certainly, son. Phoebe, how was your book reading?"

"A bit uncomfortable."

"How so?"

Phoebe pushed her potatoes around. "One of the girls implied I criticized her."

"About a book?" asked Augie.

"No, on an earlier day in her home."

Her father broke off a piece of bread from the loaf. "Did you?"

"I don't think so. At least, I hadn't intended to."

Augie thumped down his lemonade. "I bet it was one of the Simmons sisters. Jeremiah told me you visited them."

"I'd prefer not to say." Phoebe lifted her eyes to her father's. "I don't want to gossip."

"Well, Kitten, I am glad to hear it, but not every discussion about someone is gossip. Are you intending to malign her to us or gain understanding?"

"That's just it, Papa. It's hard to say. She embarrassed me in front of everyone, forcing Emily to defend me."

Amelia passed her the bread. "I doubt Emily was 'forced'. Had she agreed with the girl, she wouldn't have piped up. What was it you said?"

"I encouraged her to assume the best until we have reason to believe otherwise."

"About?"

"Isabela. This friend suggested she is deceiving us about her memory and may be running from the law."

Ernest smoothed the corner of his mustache. "She very well may be. Would that change how you treat her?"

Phoebe just stared at him for a moment. "No…I guess not."

"Just so. Not even a criminal is beyond the love of Jesus.[vi] Zacchaeus was likely a cheat."

"It's just…" Phoebe began pushing her food around again. "I now feel awkward with this friend. Maybe I should have kept silent, but you always stand up for what is right. How do you do it without offending people?"

Her mother stifled a chortle. "If you think he doesn't offend them, you haven't been paying close attention. The truth *is* offensive to anyone who wants to avoid it, but what's the alternative?"

"I guess to say nothing, but wouldn't that have reinforced her accusations? Others were listening."

"Very likely it would," replied the reverend. "My years as a professor helped modify my approach. I try to ask questions that may lead a person to reassess their suppositions. Aside from all that, though, you are now facing a more difficult problem."

"I am?"

"Yes. What will you do with your embarrassment? Do you wish to punish her or restore your relationship?"

"If I'm honest, a little of both."

"And what would that take?"

"I guess for her to acknowledge she was wrong."

"That isn't likely," her mother responded. "Though you might seek her out to say you had not meant to insult her."

"But *she* wronged *me*."

"I know, but she must have felt stung. Elsewise, she would not have retaliated?"

"Kitten, your mother is not saying the girl's comment was justified. She is suggesting you do everything in *your* power to restore the friendship. Jesus was wholly in the right, and had every reason to punish us, but what did He do, instead?"

Phoebe peered down at her lap. "'Humbled Himself…even to the point of death on the cross.'[vii]"

"Your friend may not reciprocate. You can't force her response, but as your mother asked earlier, what is your alternative?"

"To hope it goes away?"

"Your discomfort may, so *you* will feel better; but unless she repents, the two of you will still be alienated from each other."

Augie's forehead crinkled. "I don't get it. If her friend is in the wrong, why should Phoebe apologize? She'd be lying."

His father stilled his fork. "With most conflicts, fault lies on both sides. Phoebe's was not intentional, but the girl still felt hurt."

"You always say we can't choose how others feel."

"True. Offenses more often reflect the listener's heart: a desire to be seen as right, for example, or hidden insecurities or guilt—unless, of course, the speaker meant to wound. An apology may open this friend's heart—not only to Phoebe but also to Jesus."

"But all Phoebe's friends already go to church."

"Maybe so." Papa shrugged. "But that doesn't say much."

When Augie's eyes widened, Amelia added, "It's always good to hear God's Word, but folks attend church for all sorts of wrong reasons. It's their family's tradition, they desire their neighbors' good opinions. Many wish to think *themselves* good."

"They are often the hardest people to reach, son, and the likeliest to give Jesus a bad name. Whatever lies in their hearts inevitably leaks out."

"So, what do you do, Papa?" asked Phoebe.

"Love them in the very ways we've been discussing, occasionally at great cost to my pride. Once…"

A knock at the door interrupted his story.

"Ernest, you'd better answer, though I can't imagine who it would be on a Saturday night?"

Augie grinned. "Maybe another desperate lady."

While Phoebe breathed deeply to keep from retorting, she heard Foster, the church caretaker's voice.

"Sorry to bother yuh, Pastor."

"No bother. Come in."

Foster did, pressing his hat against his mid-section. "I trimmed up the bushes on the lane and was fixin' to plant spring bulbs, but my spade's missin'. I thought maybe the boy had it or the missus." He nodded to Amelia. "I seen yuh digging in your kitchen garden earlier this week."

"I cleaned and hung it right where I found it. Since you are here, would you like a piece of pie? It's blueberry, your favorite."

"Thank you, ma'am, but I'd better not. The sun's goin' down an' that spade won't find itself."

"Then I'll wrap a few slices up and you can take them with you."

"Thank yuh, kindly, Missus Farrell."

As Amelia bid Foster goodnight, Ernest glanced at Augie. He was staring down at his lap. "Son, do you know anything…"

When Sparkles sprung up and trotted toward the kitchen, Augie snatched his leash off its hook. "Why does everyone always blame me?"

"Do you want me to go after him?" offered Phoebe as the back door slammed.

"No need," replied her father. "Something seems to be eating at him. Let's give him some room."

# Chapter 12

AARON AUGER SIDLED up to Phoebe as she stepped into the church vestibule. "Good afternoon, Miss Farrell. Are you free to walk with me along the river?"

"Yes, but I need to talk with…a friend."

"No rush. I'll be at the parsonage. Your parents invited me for Sunday dinner."

"I'll be as brief as possible."

While dashing after the eldest Miss Simmons, she glanced back to see Hugh clapping Aaron on the shoulder. She was surprised neither of his English guests had joined them for the service.

"Virginia, may I speak with you a moment?"

Sarah, the youngest Simmons sister, smiled warmly before trotting toward their family's wagon where their mother waited with Megan. William stood beside it, chatting with a girl Phoebe recognized from Yancy's. Although Charles held the horses' reins, he fixed his attention on several women a stone's throw away beneath the spreading canopy of a maple tree. As Phoebe peered through the shade, she saw Lavinia clasping Isabela's hand as if Mary and Emily had just introduced them.

"I wanted to talk with you, too." Virginia lowered her voice. "I saw that you noticed."

"Noticed what?" replied Phoebe.

"What *Isabela* said yesterday. How could she talk of a man she once knew if she remembers nothing?"

Phoebe looked away. She wished to support Isabela but not with a lie. "I thought it incongruent also, though I'm still not sure she is pretending. Perhaps her memories come and go—like when I'm trying hard to supply a name I can't recall until I'm alone and elsewhere."

"Are you determined to ignore the obvious? She is hiding something; I am sure of it."

"Perhaps you're right, but why?"

"Maybe she's a thief or a murderer."

"Augie thinks she escaped from the dungeon of a wicked ruler."

Virginia smiled. She, too, had a little brother. "I hadn't considered something like that—not the dungeon part, of course, but the man she mentioned. Maybe he was her father or an older brother. Charles is never mean, but he can be high-handed." She stared down at the toe she pressed into the gravel. "My Ma once ran from my Pa. Long before you came here. Mrs. Kiker took her in, and when she came home, she brought Ruby. I've always wondered…"

"What?"

"Never mind. It's a silly idea. What could a slave woman do against a white man?"

"She could have told, and maybe that was enough. Your father depended on the Kikers for employment."

"Ginny," called William, "how long will you be?"

"Not very."

"I won't keep you. I wanted to say I am sorry. You made me realize my comments last Tuesday hurt you. That was not my intention. Will you please forgive me?"

Virginia began toying with her glove. "It's just that you always seem so…perfect. You're worse at times than Emily."

"Hurry up, Sis!" This time it was Charles.

"See what I mean? I've got to go, but maybe we could talk more soon?"

"I'd like that." As Phoebe watched her scurry to the wagon, she realized both her father and mother had been right. Virginia had not responded the way she hoped, but what might have ended as an impediment to their friendship had become an opening for something deeper. Feeling far lighter, she all but skipped toward the parsonage, humming as she went.

When she drew level with the treehouse, Augie popped his head out, waggled his eyebrows, and flashed her a mischievous grin. "Mr. Auger's over there. On the bench."

Tossing him a smile, she crested the slope and spied Aaron sitting with closed eyes, basking in the afternoon sun. "I'm sorry to have made you wait so long." She dropped onto the stone seat beside him.

"No need to be; I've been enjoying the solitude. I'm rarely alone at The Lilacs. Your talk with your friend seems to have gone well."

"Not as well as I wished, but I'm hopeful."

"Would you prefer to sit or walk?"

"Walk, if you do not mind. We are less likely to have little ears sneaking up behind us."

Rising to his feet, he held out his elbow for her hand. She took it shyly, recalling the last time they had touched. His hand had brushed hers as they stood side by side overlooking the Augers' garden. Once they reached the river, he turned parallel to the bank.

"Has your father mentioned my request? I've been waiting until we were alone to ask how you feel about it."

Phoebe glanced away. "I hardly know. I am flattered, but when I saw you last, you were assessing your intentions toward Miss Allen."

"Charlotte and I were more her father's idea than hers or mine. That is why you found us as we were, convenient companions who shared common interests, but nothing more." He slowed their steps to a standstill and studied her face. "During the short time you spent in my grandmother's home, I thought we'd begun to forge a promising bond. I won't further my suit if you find me objectionable."

"You are not objectionable in any way, it's just . . ."

He waited patiently for her to gather her thoughts.

"The events were of a particular sort to foster a feeling of closeness."

"And you fear that feeling may be false?"

"Something like that. You may find I am not who you imagine."

Aaron chuckled. "As you may also."

When she lowered her eyes, they resumed their pace, walking in companionable silence until Augie ran down the slope to tell them dinner was ready.

***

"AMELIA," CALLED ERNEST. "I'm going up to The Lilacs for a bit."

"It's an awfully long drive for you to spend such a short time. Why ever are you going—and on a Sunday evening?"

"Oh. . .just a . . .service Lavinia asked me to perform."

"So late? I cannot imagine what . . ."

Ernest cupped his wife's cheek and bent to kiss her. "No need to imagine anything, my love."

"Well, if you say so. . ."

"I should be back before you are in bed."

Augie ran up to his mother, still framed in the door, as his father climbed aboard the parsonage wagon and drove down the lane. "Where's Papa going?"

"To The Lilacs."

"Is someone sick?"

Amelia peered at her son. "Why would you ask that?"

"His smaller Bible. It was tucked into his coat pocket."

As they watched him turn onto The Pike, Amelia tilted her head. "I hope not. He didn't say."

"We can ask Phoebe when she returns from work tomorrow. She ends up hearing everything."

# Chapter 13

REVEREND FARRELL ADJUSTED his collar. "Are you ready for this, Kitten? It's one thing to further an acquaintance; quite another to do so before the world at large."

"Now, Ernest, don't go frightening Phoebe. The Nelsons are hardly 'the world.' Besides, if anything does come of this, she will want Emily to be the first to know. Speaking of secrets, it's already Tuesday and neither you nor Phoebe have told us why you went to The Lilacs Sunday evening."

"Oh—I didn't realize we were speaking of them, and our daughter does not know."

Phoebe felt relieved her mother had changed the subject. She preferred to keep her feelings about Mr. Auger to herself. She *was* eager for Emily to meet him and curious to discover what she thought, but she also felt horribly vulnerable.

Her father opened the watch he pulled from his pocket. "Mr. Auger had better come soon if we are to arrive on time. It's half-past six. Oh, that must be him now. The Kikers' carriage just turned into the lane."

"How sensible and considerate to ask if he could use it. The sky appears like it might rain."

"Where has Augie gone?" He peered up the staircase. "Son, it's time to go."

"Look, Ernest." Amelia lifted their youngest child into her husband's arms. "Lucy is cutting a new tooth."

"No wonder she's been fussy. Excuse me, dearest, he's almost at the door."

Aaron greeted each of them while they streamed out of the parsonage. "Am I late? Kitch found a nail loose in one of the horseshoes." He nodded toward the matching pair. "Let me help you up, Mrs. Farrell, Miss Farrell."

"Here, dear, take Lucy." The reverend handed back their toddler. "Augie, why don't you sit between Mr. Auger and me, so you won't wrinkle the ladies' dresses?"

The boy gladly did, entertaining both men with a fishing story. Phoebe took the chance to study Aaron. He was far better dressed than her father, who wore his coats until the elbows frayed and paid no attention to fashion. If Aaron noticed, he did not let on. Instead, he engaged her parents with respectful interest and Augie with humor.

Would their little brothers like each other? They were vastly different. The younger was all affection and tenderness and the elder all roughhousing and adventure. She loved them both but feared William would find Augie overwhelming. How would her mother and Aaron's Aunt Margaret feel about each other? Mama, she was confident, would search for common ground and if she could not find any, she would still offer his aunt her friendship. How would Aunt Margaret respond to Mama?

Both she and his Uncle Oliver had presented sour dispositions while Phoebe worked for Aaron's grandmother last yuletide. Oliver had sharply protested her presence in their home. What might he say if she returned as its mistress?

Before she could ruminate further, they were rolling down the long lane beside the river and stopping so the driver could fold back the wrought iron gates. Emily hurried to greet them, her cheeks flushed from the effort and her light brown chignon threatening to come loose, but when she noticed a stranger descending from the carriage, she stepped backward and smoothed her hair into place. Phoebe thought she looked beautiful.

"Where's Papa Nelson?" asked Augie. Before Emily answered, he bolted toward the water.

"Please excuse his manners," Phoebe's father pleaded. Stepping aside while their guest assisted his daughter, he offered his wife a hand. "He's been eager to see the colonel all day."

"No offense taken, Pastor Farrell. I cannot blame him."

"How sweet you are, Emily." Amelia's smile held obvious affection. "You are just how I imagine your grandmother to have been at your age."

Emily blushed profusely. "Thank you. I hope I will not disappoint you as I age."

"Mr. Auger," began the reverend, "this is our daughter's dear friend, Emily Nelson."

Aaron took the hand she held toward him. "It's a pleasure to meet you. Your grandparents have a beautiful estate." He peered up at the tall pillars supporting the home's roof and beyond to the pasture. "What do you call it?"

"River Bend, for its setting. See, the river turns there." She indicated the spot where Augie and the colonel had just been standing. "Grandpa must have caught us a catfish for dinner. He and Augie are walking back toward the kitchen." As her eyes followed them to the side of the house, the front door swooshed open.

"Welcome," her grandmother called from the porch. "Do come in. The first course is on the table, and Sally will have that catfish fried in no time at all." She stepped aside to allow them to enter. "You must be Hilda's grandson."

Aaron shot her a questioning gaze. "Yes. Did you know her?"

"Quite well. We came out during the same season, a summer before either of us married."

"And the colonel?"

"I don't believe he ever had the pleasure."

"Mama Nelson," said Phoebe, "you never told me you knew Mrs. Auger."

"You never asked." Though her blue eyes sparkled, she crossed the foyer to the parlor. "Mr. Auger, this is Isabela, our houseguest."

The petite young woman laid aside her book, rising from the settee to extend her hand. "You are an acquaintance of Miss Farrell, no?"

"A friend, I hope." As he bowed over Isabela's hand, he glanced at Phoebe, but she did not notice. She was busy admiring the blonde tendrils that framed Isabela's kitten-like face. How she kept them so perfectly curled, Phoebe could not imagine. They had stayed that way even while she was passed out in the parsonage.

As Augie and Colonel Nelson tromped in from outside, Emily wound her arm through Phoebe's and drew her a scant distance away. "Is this the...friend from Pennsylvania you described to me? The one who assisted Matthew Bentley?"

"No." Phoebe whispered. "That was someone else. Mr. Auger manages the bequest his grandmother left for me."

"Then you aren't . . .?"

Isabela drew their attention, slipping her arm through Aaron's as they walked through the pocket doors to the dining room. "They are an enchanting pair of girls."

"This is the first I've met Miss Nelson."

"She is the kindest, most even-tempered young woman, though she is less inclined to speak than her dark-haired friend. Whether from a natural reserve or a judicious temperament, I have yet to uncover."

"Have you known the Nelsons many years?"

"Oh, no, not so very long. Ah, here we are. I believe Mary—Mrs. Nelson—planned for you to sit there, to her right, while I sit on the other end of the table, next to her husband."

Once she and the others had taken their places, Colonel Nelson gave thanks, and his wife passed Aaron a relish tray.

"You have a beautiful home, Mrs. Nelson. Are these vegetables from your garden?"

"All but the asparagus. Try it. It's pickled." She passed him a basket of cornbread once he had moved a few stalks to his plate.

"My compliments to your cook."

"Our Sally is a treasure."

"I see you do not keep . . ."

"Slaves? Gary and I don't agree with the practice, though we are indebted to Lavinia's cook for our cornbread recipe."

Amelia put a square of it on her bread plate. "Our family had never eaten cornbread before moving south. Ernest, please pass me the slaw."

"Here you go, dear. Between new food choices and less demand to walk, my waistbands are beginning to feel a bit snug."

"I can easily see how that might happen." Aaron nodded. "Although we own horses, most places in Allentown are within a comfortable walk from our home."

Phoebe felt a toe nudge her slipper beneath the table. Emily, seated directly opposite, flicked her eyes toward Augie. He was sitting still, which was remarkable, grinning blissfully at Isabela while his head listed to one side. When Phoebe opened her mouth to comment, Emily kicked her so sharply she snapped it shut. Her friend was right. To tease him would be unkind, and no one could fault his taste in women. Isabela's eyes were large and her eyebrows, of a far darker shade then her golden hair, accentuated them perfectly.

"Our estate borders a delightful…" When Isabela trailed off, pressing a napkin to her mouth, Colonel Nelson plunked down his fork.

"Please . . . go on."

"Oh . . . um, I fear I have lost the trail to my thoughts again. You must excuse me."

"You were describing your . . ."

"Now Gary," cautioned his wife. "You know Dr. Stillman asked us not to press."

"Ah, Mary, you are kindness itself, but I do not mind—and I remember now. I was saying how invitingly the river touches the two sides of your estate. I enjoy watching the sun gleam across its ripples, though I am afraid of stepping too close to the edge." Her eyes leaped from Mrs. Nelson to Sally, who had carried into the dining room a heavy cut-glass tray. "Oh, the fish smells marvelous. What did you tell me it is called?"

"Catfish."

Augie straightened. "I helped catch it! If you want, after dinner, I'll walk you alongside the bank and show you all the best places to fish. You can hold onto my arm."

"Ah, Augie. First, you give me a new name and now you will keep me safe. You may be your sister's little brother, but to me you are a young man."

Augie beamed, but his father interrupted. "Son, let's allow our hosts to devise the after-dinner plans."

"A walk by the river would be lovely," answered Mary. "We thought it might rain, but it appears to have passed. With as dry as it's been lately, the bank should be firm."

While the conversation moved to other topics, Phoebe noticed Aaron was absorbing Emily's attention. Her lips curved sweetly, her eyes filled with light, and he looked as happily occupied as she was. Phoebe felt pleased that he enjoyed the Nelsons, Emily especially. If their acquaintance eventually progressed to something permanent, she hoped he would welcome frequent visits. She would certainly need a friend. As her musings returned to his home on Chew Street, she began feeling closed in.

"So, Mr. Auger." Colonel Nelson gazed eagerly at him. "Tell us about Hugh's other guests."

"I am afraid I must disappoint you, sir. I barely know either. You can form your own opinion at the end of the month. Mrs. Kiker has arranged a ball to introduce them."

"And to introduce you, too," replied Mary. Her gaze skipped from him to Sally, who had brought out a large bowl of trifle for dessert, and then to her houseguest.

"Isabela, you must come also. It would do you a world of good to get into the company of other young people."

Isabela dropped her napkin, nearly bumping heads with Augie as he bent to scoop it up. "Oh, no. I could not intrude."

"It's no intrusion," answered the colonel. "We are in and out of each other's pockets all the time."

Emily leaned forward. "Clara invited you last Saturday."

"Oh, yes. I did not connect the two. So kind of her, but may I give you an answer closer to the day?"

While Phoebe listened, she felt sympathy for Isabela. She keenly disliked a sea of new faces, preferring to meet people one at a time.

"I'll be there," offered Augie, showing sensitivity his sister was not aware he possessed.

"Well then, *if* I go, I will save you a dance."

# Chapter 14

AMELIA AND PHOEBE sat in the parlor the next evening after supper, darning holes in the family's socks. "I don't know how he does it."

"Who, Mama?"

"Augie. How does he make so many holes? You'd think we don't supply him shoes."

Phoebe's dimples twitched. "I once found him outside without them in the snow."

"Oh, that boy! You outgrew yours before they needed mending. I do love him, though." She grew a bit wistful. "Sons and daughters each have separate charms. I don't know what I'll do without you."

As her mother grew quiet, Phoebe raised her eyes. "We won't face that for a good while."

"I love you dearly and would never stand in your way, but Pennsylvania is so far. You might as well be back in Princeton. I will see you scarcely twice a year. I must admit, though, he is a very nice man, so solid and so pleasant." She chuckled. "Just listen to me. I sound like the mother in one of those novels you are reading." When Phoebe did not respond, Amelia laid down her needle. "You have grown awfully quiet. Have I said the wrong thing?"

"No, Mama, not at all. It's just…I have been doing a lot of thinking."

"About your Mr. Auger?"

"Not him so much as…I don't think I'm ready to leave you and Papa."

"I felt the same when your father began to court me. I was barely older than you are now."

"Did you love him?"

"Oh, yes! He was and still is the most interesting and considerate man I've ever known, always thinking of others. To live without him seemed unthinkable."

Phoebe pressed her lips into a thin, tightly closed smile.

"How do you feel about Mr. Auger?"

"I don't know. He is all the things you and father have said and handsome besides. Still, I keep remembering how lonely I felt at while in Allentown. To leave everyone I dearly love for a man I barely know…Lucy will probably forget who I am."

"Is that all that is bothering you?"

"No." Phoebe paused to weigh what she might say. Were she to describe the interactions she had observed within Aaron's family last winter, she would risk tainting her parents' opinions. "I would not fit. Mr. Auger's family are leaders in their community, entertaining businessmen and dignitaries locally and abroad."

"Then you would be a great asset to him. You would plan those parties and run his household, just as you have helped Lavinia do. Working at The Lilacs will have prepared you well."

"He doesn't need any of that. He has a housekeeper to manage the staff and plan their events, and his Aunt Margaret to approve the menus."

Though Amelia raised her eyes, she lowered her chin until it nearly rested on her chest. "If you were up to your elbows in soiled nappies, as many women are once they have children, you would be grateful for a staff, particularly a laundress. Do you feel…inferior to the society you would meet?"

"No, though many of their friends might think me so. During the two weeks I was there, I ate with the family but moved freely between upstairs and downstairs. Given a choice, I preferred the servants' company every time."

Her mother chuckled. "I am not surprised."

"Then you see my difficulty. If Aaron and I were to invite friends for dinner, we could invite only *his*. Mine would be serving us!"

"Could you not learn to like them?"

Phoebe puffed out a gust of air. "I am quite fond of Tandy Bentley and her husband Matthew. You may remember them from our first Lilac Ball. But I would be mortified to have the people I care most about waiting on me hand and foot. To idle my days away and spend my evenings discussing Godey's latest fashions would be torturous."

Amelia could not help but smile. "You are the first young woman I've met who may refuse a suitor *because* he is too rich. You are so like your father, and like me, frankly. That sort of talk would put me to sleep."

"I suppose if I felt about Aaron as you did for Papa, I might not care about the rest."

"You are sure you don't?"

"I might in time, were he the only factor to consider, but how are we to manage that? He cannot stay at The Lilacs indefinitely, and the thought of returning to his home fills me with dread."

"It sounds as if you may know your answer. If you are quite sure, you had best tell him soon. If you give him a chance to become deeply attached, you will only hurt him more."

"But, Mama, how do I express any of this to him? The match's advantages are all on my side."

"As the world sees them, yes, but you have more to offer than can be measured in dollars and cents."

"You are my Mama. It's natural for you to love me, but I don't want to be foolish. He may be the only man who will ever pursue me."

"Only if the Lord wishes it so. Why don't we find your father and we will pray."

"Do you mind if we pray by ourselves? I am not ready to speak about my feelings with him or anyone else just yet."

# Chapter 15

AS PHOEBE'S FRIENDS gathered in River Bend's parlor on Saturday, Isabela opened *Sense and Sensibility*, the next Austen novel they planned to discuss. She glanced at each girl in succession. "I have a confession to make."

Virginia and Megan Simmons leaned forward in their seats. Clara Kiker twirled her dark hair. Lisa White and Phoebe settled their plates of petits fours on their laps, and Emily sipped her tea.

"I have been reading ahead, and in each of Miss Austen's novels, one of you has supplied me with a portrait of a character. We have already agreed that Lisa is Jane Bennet."

"Who am I?" asked Megan.

"You are Catherine Morland, with her youth and sweet temper."

"I do not remember her. Was she one of Lizzy's younger sisters from *Pride and Prejudice*?"

"Ah, no. Though she possesses an imagination most vivid, she is not so silly as those girls were. I forgot that we have not yet read Northanger Abbey. She is its heroine."

"And me?" asked Virginia.

"I would prefer to hear who *you* feel most like. It is not always appealing to learn how someone else sees you, even if she intends it as a compliment; and many of the novels' heroines share common elements: loyalty, intelligence, good sense, and a great deal of vivacity. Afterward, I would like to know which of Austen's men would suit each of you best."

"That part's easy." Megan sparkled. "Mr. Darcy. He is handsome and oh so rich, though now that I have met that Mr. Whitcomb, I am not so sure."

"Who is Mr. Whitcomb?" asked Isabela.

"One of our investors," answered Clara. "They arrived with my brother from New York at the beginning of the month. Last week, I compared him to Lizzy's first thoughts of Mr. Darcy."

"Thursday evening," added Virginia, "while our family was eating dinner with Clara's, he could not be bothered with anyone but his hosts and friends. My mother and Meg tried to converse with him, but his answers were so short, both Clara's father and brother appeared cross with him. It takes a lot to ruffle their feathers, wouldn't you agree?"

"Yes," admitted Clara. "I cannot recall the last time I saw either of them so embarrassed."

"Maybe this guest," offered Emily, "is simply reserved. Not all men have the charm of his friend."

"Whose friend?" asked Virginia. "Darcy's or Whitcomb's?"

"Either." Megan giggled. "Now that I've met him, I agree with what Phoebe told us last Saturday. He is so like Bingley that Miss Austen might have styled the character after him."

"Which makes him," added Clara, "an equally appealing catch."

Virginia creased her brow. "I thought *you* would favor Captain Wentworth."

"I do." Clara dropped her eyes to her tea. "But though Anne Elliot and I have much in common, we also have our differences. I would far prefer a mannerly, handsome husband with a fine fortune to growing old alone."

"Is Anne Elliot the character," asked Lisa, "you feel matches you best?"

Phoebe was surprised to see Clara redden. "Undoubtedly."

"But Anne is so plain," protested Megan.

"Not plain—despairing." Isabela's eyes filled with sympathy. "Anne feels deeply for a man her family refuses to consider. It is hard, Megan, is it not, to see beyond the obvious, though I, too, would have cast Clara as one of Austen's beauties. Perhaps Emma."

"Who do you see yourself as?" asked Phoebe.

Isabela paused in thought. "I am at a disadvantage. I have only vague impressions of who I am. Perhaps Maryanne since her heart was so broken. And you, Emily? Who would you choose?"

Emily flushed, though Phoebe could not tell if her thoughts disturbed her or she disliked gaining the center of attention. "I felt the most like Fanny Price, but I would not wish to marry Edmund Bertram. He was too easily led."

"Who would suit you better?"

Emily considered for a moment. "Mr. Knightly or Darcy's cousin, Colonel Fitzwilliam. Both are men of integrity and intelligence, even-tempered, and consistently kind."

"What about you, Phoebe?" Clara slid her a teasing glance. "Who is most like your Mr. Auger?"

"Mr. Auger?" asked Isabela. "Isn't he the smart-looking gentleman who accompanied you to dinner the other evening? So charming and gallant."

As all eyes turned in Phoebe's direction, she wished she could sink behind the settee. "He was a guest of my whole family, but if I am to describe him, I must steal one of Emily's answers. He is very like Mr. Knightly or Darcy's cousin."

Clara tried to squelch her grin. "And would Colonel Fitzwilliam suit your fancy?"

"I hardly know. I like many things about.…Colonel Fitzwilliam. He is self- controlled, not tossed about or drawn away with emotions like Edmund or even Mr. Darcy. But I am torn over my favorite. I admire both Colonel Brandon and Captain Wentworth for the same reasons: their faithfulness."

"But Colonel Brandon and Captain Wentworth are completely different," Virginia exclaimed. "Brandon is all dullness and duty; Captain Wentworth all dash and daring."

"Ginny," said Megan, "you sound as if Mr. Wentworth is your favorite."

"Oh no. Any dog is faithful. I prefer a man who is diverting, who yearns for adventure—a Willoughby to my Marianne—though with a more secure fortune. If I can't have him, I will sift through the pages of another author."

"But, Virginia," responded Lisa, "if his fidelity, like Willoughby's, depended on his fortune, how could you ever trust him? What if, someday, you ceased being an asset? Would he begin to search elsewhere for what he wants?"

"I suppose that would depend on whether he genuinely loved me."

"Which would?" asked Emily. "His fidelity or your standing by him?"

"Both." Virginia lifted her chin. "If he truly loved me, he would not waver."

"Then," asked Clara, "what does that say about Willoughby's depth of love?"

While her sister paused, fumbling with a cuff, Megan sat up straighter. "He loved Marianne, truly. He confessed as much to Elinor."

Isabela's sigh was filled with regret. "Miss Austen demonstrates in her books what youth and inexperience would rather deny. If he had truly loved her, his actions would have said so. Instead, they announced his true love was his pocket."

"I know I am jumping ahead again," replied Emily, "but you have reminded me of Fanny Price's mother. I had the impression Austen wished to steer young women away from imprudent matches."

"Perhaps," admitted Lisa, "she wishes to acquaint us with a variety of pitfalls we might confront. I have found the books full of men ill-using women and women who might aim to do the same. Mary Crawford for example, of Mansfield Park, desires Edmund for his fortune alone."

Isabela turned to look at Phoebe, who was sitting on the other end of her settee. "You've grown quiet."

"I am considering what everyone has said and must agree with Lisa, or rather, Miss Austen. Ditches appear to exist on both sides of the road that are equally easy to fall into. I wish to marry a man I feel for deeply, yet, the love Fanny's mother bore for her husband could not feed her children. I suppose if I marry a man whom I can both respect and admire, the level of my feelings for him will deepen; but the level of a man's income can't guarantee his character."

"What do you advise?" asked Emily.

"I'm not in a position to advise anyone, but I am coming to the same conclusion I suspect Miss Austen did: that similarity of character and purpose in life are better predictors of marital happiness than either wealth or passion."

"I wonder," began Lisa, "if God had something like that in mind when He created Eve for Adam—not just a female but one that was well-suited to the task God assigned him."

"Do you mean like Priscilla and Aquila?" asked Emily.

"In what way?"

"As I read of them this morning, I began to think how ill-suited Aquilla and I would be. Priscilla appears to have travelled with him, helping him ply his trade while telling people of Jesus.[viii] While I admire her and wish to serve God's purposes, I am a homebody, which prompted me to think about other women the book of Acts portrays. Some had to be more like me, perhaps Lydia, who invited Paul and his companions to stay with her, or Dorcas, who provided clothing for those in need."

"Like you have done for me," commented Isabela.

"We are enjoying having you here. You have not yet said who you would be or like to marry."

"In this, I must disappoint you. Like Emma before she loved Knightly, I am determined never to marry anyone."

# Chapter 16

WHEN PHOEBE PEEKED out the front window, the entire county appeared to be crowded onto The Lilacs' tall porch or waiting on the stairs leading up to it. She feared Jubal might grow hoarse from announcing new arrivals before the evening ended. How did this week fly by so quickly? She had barely had a chance to speak with Aaron.

Unlike her first dance at The Lilacs, she had helped plan and execute this ball's details. Her hands were still sore from clipping roses, and her thumb throbbed from a thorn-prick. Much to her relief, the young women included in the Nelsons' weekly gathering had been happy to cancel today.

Mitilde and the kitchen help had been cooking and baking all week, eliciting a continual symphony of growling stomachs. Her husband, Kitch, had flung wide the connecting doors between the parlor and dining room and lined them with every settee and chair he could find. Through the doors to the rear of the home lay a tented stone patio, constructed for the occasion, onto which footmen had carried the lengthy dining room table. They had then strategically stacked polished silver and starched napkins within the guests' easy reach, though the Kikers would not serve supper until well into the evening.

"Do you think we will have enough room?" Hugh leaned over her, the placket of his coat brushing her shoulder.

"Only because we can spill out into the gardens. I'm glad you came home in October. Any earlier and the humidity might be unbearable; any later, and we would have risked frost."

"I see the mystery woman is making an appearance."

"Yes, though Mary and Emily had quite a time persuading her to come."

"Will I provoke Aaron's wrath if I tell you how lovely you look tonight?"

Phoebe turned toward him. "You have nothing to fear in that respect.

"I had thought you attached to him. He is an admirable man. Are you having doubts?"

"I have yet to convince myself I am suited to the role of the *squire's wife*, though I heartily agree with your assessment of him."

"Then why break his heart?"

"I doubt there is any chance of that; at least, I hope not. From what I have observed, he never rushes headlong into anything."

"What would his late grandmother say?"

Phoebe dimpled. "I have not yet decided to turn him away, but she made the option possible."

"How?"

"In her will, she left me a generous stipend."

Hugh's eyebrows shot upward. "Why? You only stayed with her a few weeks."

"They were long enough for us to become attached. She set it up to prevent me from marrying from fear of want."

"You will lack nothing as his wife, and wealth affords opportunities to help those less fortunate."

"You think I should marry so I can be more charitable?"

"Many have wed for lesser reasons and found their lives fulfilling. Take Mother for example."

"Your mother loved your father from the onset. I have heard her say so."

"She still does, and marriage to him has placed her well to accomplish certain…goals…she couldn't have without being mistress of The Lilacs."

The glint in his eye declared he knew his mother's secret and might have abetted her.[ix] Still, though Phoebe longed to speak with him openly, the risk she might be mistaken was too great. "I was not raised with wealth and feel the differences keenly."

"Such as?"

"Your mother's proficiency at hosting the whole county and her hopes for Clara. If Aaron and I were blessed with children, I'd as soon have them marry our maids or stable hands, provided the kingdom of God were their priorities. He will certainly make the *right* woman an estimable partner but look at me."

"I am." Hugh's lips curved warmly. "That salmon pink highlights your…coloring."

"Thank you." She tucked her head down, flushing as his gaze took in her bare shoulders. He did not appear to recognize his sister's cast-off.

"You are wearing my brooch."

Her fingers touched the single piece of jewelry pinned to the ribbon above her collarbone. "I do so often."

Hugh's eyes filled with something she could not place. "The loss will be Aaron's if you decide against him. I cannot think of a single woman with a truer heart."

"Then you have overlooked a much finer one than mine." She slid her eyes to the window and nodded toward a young woman on the porch. "But I'm afraid your mother was right."

Hugh leaned in close as he followed her gaze, then he suddenly stood alert. "That's Emily!"

Phoebe looked over her shoulder and smiled. "Haven't you seen her since you returned? You had mentioned a present you brought her."

"I meant to give it to her tonight."

"Considering the setting, don't you think she might assume a particular meaning?"

"I hadn't thought of that."

"Well, you may not have awakened to the treasure she is, but others have." She indicated the unfamiliar well-dressed young man she had been watching. He had purposefully made his way over to Allison and John Wilson, who had then introduced him to the Nelsons. The colonel was quite clearly not his aim.

"Graham is wasting no time."

"You know him?"

"The Jamisons are among the richest landholders in Richmond. He has recently become the governor's aide."

"Then she would suit him perfectly, and 'it is a truth universally acknowledged, that a single man in possession of a good fortune must be in want of a wife.'[x]"

As he stiffened his lips into a hard line, Clara, looking exquisite in her pale-yellow tarlatan, swept up behind them. "Here you are, Hugh! Mother sent me. We can't form the reception line without you. We *are* holding this ball in your honor."

Hugh slid her a sideways glance. "In my honor, yes, but for your benefit. I am coming. Phoebe, save me the first dance."

"Aaron has secured it already." She peered back out the window.

"All right, the second." His eyes twinkled as Clara pulled him toward the foyer.

***

WHILE THE MUSICIANS were finishing the first set, Emily swished up to Phoebe and Aaron with Hugh trailing a few footfalls behind her. "You look radiant, Phoebe."

The two young women kissed each other's cheeks. "So do you. The color of your gown reminds me of the maple's changing leaves outside my window, not quite yellow but too vivid and gold to call apricot."

"You look lovely also. Did you see Augie and Isabela dancing?"

"Yes." Phoebe dimpled. "I hope her toes are not too damaged."

"She has certainly won his heart."

As Aaron held out his hand toward Phoebe, Hugh stepped closer. "Sorry, old friend. Miss Farrell promised me the second set."

Aaron inclined his head toward Emily. "I had hoped to dance with Miss Nelson also, if she will grant me the honor."

"Of course," replied Emily casually, but the bloom of her cheeks announced she was delighted.

Once Hugh led Phoebe away, he pulled her into the string of dancers. "If I weren't the guest of honor, Emily might have turned me down. Graham Jamison was already trying to engage her."

"As he likely will for the third dance. He is watching her as we speak."

"I may need to pull out Father's dueling pistols."

Phoebe's steps almost faltered.

"Don't look so horrified." He laughed. "I am not serious. Who knew she would blossom into such a beauty?"

"Your mother, for one, and possibly Clara. She's teased you all year, something she would not have dared to do had she not wished you to court Emily."

"I wish Father would relent about Charles and Clara. I've forgiven Charles for thrashing me,[xi] why can't he?"

"I don't know your father well enough to answer that question, but forgiveness might not be the key. Your father dotes on Clara. Charles likely lost his trust. Would you give your prize possession to someone you feared might destroy it in a fit of temper?"[xii]

"No." Hugh suddenly sobered. "I hadn't considered that. Miss Farrell, you'd best be careful."

"Around Charles?" Phoebe crinkled her brow.

"No." His eyes danced merrily. "With me. I just may try to win you for myself."

As Phoebe flushed, the dancers swirled them away from each other, making a reply impossible for the moment.

"You are far too handsome for me, Hugh."

"Then you do not give your features sufficient credit."

"I am practical. You are a cardinal; I am a titmouse."

The dance steps parted and brought them back together.

"The bluish-gray birds with the bright black eyes? They are my favorites."

Phoebe laughed. If this was what flirting felt like, she decidedly enjoyed it. "Both birds hold their own charms, but they are not well-matched."

"Are they *so* dissimilar? They are the same shape and have those pointed little tufts atop their heads."

"Yes, but there the similarity ends. Besides…"

Two dancers split them apart, joining their hands with Hugh's and Phoebe's.

"You were saying?"

"If I am ill-suited to manage the Augers' staff, I am even less so to manage an enslaved one. I would make friends with each and set them all free."

"Now…" He leaned so close she could feel his breath. "…of whom might that remind me?"[xiii]

Phoebe was as surprised by his remark as by the heat flooding her cheeks. He *was* the most attractive man she had ever encountered and extremely attentive, but his annoyance with Emily's admirer surely belied any serious intentions. Still, it renewed her questions about exactly how much his father knew of Lavinia's pursuits. Could a man be perceptive and intelligent in his business practices but utterly unaware of the proceedings within his home?

As the musicians rested their bows, Phoebe fully expected Hugh to seek a different partner. Instead, he stayed by her side until they heard the next chords.

"Ah, a reel. Will you do me the pleasure?"

"Tongues will wag. Hadn't you better ask Virginia or Megan? Mr. Jamison has succeeded with Emily and your mother is conversing with Judge Pennybacker's wife."

"If they must wag, let them. They will also wag if you dance too often with Aaron. Besides, he has secured a dance with…what did you call the mystery woman?"

"Isabela."

Grabbing Phoebe's hands, he pulled her into the dance's steps—too lively for conversation—and by the time the reel ended beside Clara and Mr. Pinder, their sides ached from effort and laughter.

"Wesley." Hugh clapped the fair Englishman on his back. "Are you enjoying our country dance?"

Mr. Pinder tossed his partner a shy glance. "I have been up until now, but I'm afraid I might be rude to your guest if I continue to monopolize your sister." As if he had only then noticed Phoebe's presence, he inclined his head toward her. "Miss Farrell, will you do me the honors?"

Phoebe felt so happy for Clara that she sloughed off the slight. "I would be delighted, sir, if you will just let me catch my breath."

Clara looked from them to her brother, but she found only Hugh's back. He was already claiming Emily's next dance. Aaron appeared in his wake, but Mr. Pinder began leading Phoebe away before she discovered whether he sought her or Hugh's sister.

# Chapter 17

AS THEY PERFORMED the first steps, the edges of Mr. Pinder's blue eyes crinkled. "For a Vicar's daughter, you are astonishingly light on your feet."

Phoebe's dimples started twitching. "I do tear myself away occasionally from reading my father's sermon notes."

"Forgive me." The skin above his cravat reddened. "My remark sounded abominably rude. I intended it as a compliment. Our vicar's daughters back home are unsophisticated by comparison. Experience has taught me to guard my toes."

"Then, I thank you. Have you been enjoying Virginia?"

"Yes. I find such rustic simplicity appealing."

As his eyes wandered to Clara, Phoebe questioned whether he meant the commonwealth or their younger hostess. The locals thought Clara the height of social acumen. "Your manor must be grand by comparison."

"It's comfortable enough, though more formal."

"In what way?"

"It lacks The Lilacs' cozy size, and all the hedges are manicured for symmetry."

The steps interposed others for several beats.

"And Mr. Whitcomb? Is his estate as formal?"

"Here comes the man now. If he is like most men, he will enjoy describing it in detail. I believe the musicians are finishing this set. Would you like something to drink?"

"Thank you, no. I need to see if Mrs. Kiker needs any help."

As Pinder bowed, Phoebe scanned the room for Lavinia, but the press of the crowd was so thick, she moved barely a foot.

"Well, Whitcomb," she heard Pinder saying, "are you enjoying yourself?"

"Hardly. I never put stock in the descriptions of our former colonies, but these past weeks have me convinced."

"Of what?"

"They were populated by England's dregs. Their governor—that tall chap next to the district judge—reminds me of my stable manager. Kiker abandoned me to them and his vicar."

"Then, when the musicians start up again, you will need to invite one of the young ladies for a dance."

"I suppose I should ask one of our hostesses. It wouldn't do for me to offend a new business partner. Who is the petite woman in the apple green gown—the one with the gold ringlets?" Whitcomb nodded toward Isabela's back as she twirled beneath Asa Kiker's arm.

"I'd not noticed her. Ask Miss Farrell, just there to the right of us. She will know."

Whitcomb arched his brows. "The vicar's daughter? I'd just as soon you poke my eye with a sharp stick."

The glimpse Phoebe caught of Pinder's blue eyes softened the sting. They held pique and surprise. "You do her a great injustice. She converses as pleasingly as she dances."

"I just spent a very dull half hour listening to her father…"

A break in the crowd allowed her to inch out of earshot. She did not care what Mr. Whitcomb thought of her, but she could not endure to hear her father spoken of in such a way. Spotting Lavinia with her mother and Aunt Allison, she edged toward the room's perimeter, out onto the veranda, and back through an open window.

"Why, Phoebe." Lavinia took her arm. "Are you enjoying yourself?"

"I am, but I thought I'd check to see if you need me to do anything."

"Aren't you dear! Everything is in place. Amelia, your daughter is a continual delight."

Amelia smiled proudly. "We think so."

"Mama, where is Lucy?"

"Little Sarah Simmons has her. Such a thoughtful girl."

"Speaking of Lucy, Auntie Allison, I've noticed Lisa and Jordan did not come."

Allison's dark eyes sparkled. "They are home with their new arrival: Luke Joshua."

"That's wonderful! You must be thrilled. May we visit?"

"I wouldn't just yet, but in a week or two."

"Phoebe." Amelia touched her daughter's arm. "I feel so bad for Hugh's dark-haired English friend. He's had little success securing partners. Do go stand where he can see you are available. He has been alone most the night."

"I was just there, Mama, and overheard him say he would not dance."

"He is in mourning," explained Lavinia. "If he were not a guest in our home, he would not have come."

"I am sorry to hear it," replied Allison. "He is so young to be widowed."

Phoebe flicked Lavinia a grateful glance. Though she cared not to repeat his cutting remarks, she would rather sit out for the rest of the evening than to partner with him. The similarity Megan Simmons drew between him and Mr. Darcy missed the mark. Darcy was proud of his station in society, but his housekeeper's comments at Pemberley assured readers that he had never truly been mean.[xiv]

While she waited for another break in the crush, she spotted Isabela with Charles and wondered who introduced them. She supposed Mrs. Nelson, who was eager to make the evening agreeable to her charge. Charles seemed equally eager to engage Isabela, but Phoebe soon began to question his motives. Over her golden hair, he was watching Pinder, who had managed to navigate his way back to Clara who was smiling up at him as if he were the only man in the room.

"Miss Farrell." Mr. Whitcomb touched her elbow. "Pinder assures me you are an excellent dancer."

She clasped the hand he held out, dimpling so deeply he tilted his lips slightly in return. If he took her reaction for pleasure, he was mistaken. His request was so like a scene in the book she had just been contemplating, she was trying not to descend into a fit of giggles.[xv]

After the promenade, Whitcomb broke his silence. "I see Pinder doesn't exaggerate. Tell me, who is the woman by the window with the Kikers' foreman? I noticed you watching them for some minutes."

"She is a guest of the Nelsons'." Phoebe had no intention of filling in the details, though she was not sure why. Perhaps he had offended her more deeply than she admitted to herself, or perhaps what Virginia had suspected had merit. *Something* had driven Isabela to the parsonage doorstep, though Phoebe doubted she ran from the law. "Colonel Nelson is the very pleasant older gentleman standing by the pillar with my father. Shall I introduce you, or would you prefer to meet the lady herself?"

He looked abashed, though had the steps not brought their faces close to each other, she would not have noticed. "Perhaps later. Where did you say she is from?"

"I didn't." Phoebe remained tight-lipped, glad they would soon need to gambol down the line.

"What do you know about her?"

"Very little."

"Then when did you meet?"

"Not long before I first met you and Mr. Pinder. Do you miss your late wife terribly?" The question was far too personal, but his keen interest in Isabela contradicted his earlier refusal to break his mourning.

"My..."

"Your adamant objection to attending this ball roused my...admiration...that day at breakfast. I have little experience of the larger world, but I've read some husbands are not so...attached...to their wives as you were to yours."

"I prefer not to discuss the subject. If you will pardon me, I need to speak with a man I see."

Whisking them away from the dancers, he strode out the door adjusting the collar around his neck.

# Chapter 18

PHOEBE FELT STUNNED to be abandoned mid-set, but before she had time to grow embarrassed, William Simmons, Charles's younger brother, slipped a hand about her waist and swirled her back into the dancers.

"I'm sorry for grabbing you so unceremoniously, but I saw a certain look in that Englishman's eye and am determined to avoid him."

"No apology needed. You have rescued me, truly. Are you enjoying your job with Mr. Yancy?"

William's smile was a replica of Charles's. "Far more than farming."

"What is Mr. Whitcomb pestering you about?"

"The woman he's searching for. You do not remember? I mentioned it when I saw you last."

"Mr. Whitcomb?" She missed a step. "I had assumed you meant Mr. Pinder."

"I'm not sure of his name. He never introduced himself."

"Have you discovered anything?"

"No, and the next time I saw him, I gave him back his sovereign. Frankly, I don't like being paid to snoop."

"I do not blame you."

As the piece of music was nearing its end, William guided them toward his sisters. "Would you like something to drink?"

"Please."

Sarah echoed Phoebe's response. Lucy was asleep on her shoulder, pinning her in place, while Virginia and Megan huddled together.

"If Charles asks Isabela for another dance," whispered Megan, "he may cause a scandal."

"I don't think he cares," answered Virginia. "He seems determined to match Clara and her Englishman turn for turn. *They* are the pair creating a scandal."

"It's only natural for Clara to dance with him. He is staying in her home."

"Four dances is beyond mannerly, and what of her other guest? With him, she hasn't made the slightest effort."

"Mr. Whitcomb," answered Phoebe, "has recently been widowed and prefers not to dance."

Virginia slid her an arch glance. "Except with you?"

His motives puzzled Phoebe also, but she had nothing other than suspicions to offer. As she shrugged, one subject of their gossip stepped toward them, flushing Virginia's neck, and nearly sending Megan into a swoon.

"Mr. Pinder," said Phoebe. "May I introduce Charles Simmons' sisters? This is Miss Virginia Simmons, Megan, and Sarah. Their brother and mine are playing outside."

"It is my pleasure." He bowed. "Though I've met them already. They are friends of Clara's who visited The Lilacs with their mother one evening. Miss Simmons, would you care to dance?"

Megan was attempting to stifle a giggle while Virginia dipped a little lower than necessary and smiled. As he swept her into the parlor, Aaron took his place.

"You have been well-occupied, Phoebe."

"As have you."

"May I accompany you to supper? Lavinia said they will serve it after the next set."

"It will be my pleasure."

"Then I will collect you by the doors to the patio. Miss Megan, would you like to dance?" As the girl's cheeks turned pink, she placed her fingers over Aaron's.

Emily swished forward and grasped Phoebe by the hands. "It's horribly warm in here. Will you join me on the veranda?" Assuming the answer, she tugged her toward the door. "I've been so eager to speak with you." Her eyes were alight with pleasure. "I am having the most wonderful evening."

"I noticed Hugh has asked you to dance with him several times."

Emily looked away, leaving Phoebe to guess what she might be thinking. "The Kikers have invited so many fine gentlemen tonight. I had not realized how full our county is with them, though I think your Mr. Auger is the most interesting of them all."

"Everyone keeps calling him 'my Mr. Auger,' but we are honestly not a couple. We are simply becoming reacquainted to confirm our first impressions."

"And have you?"

"It is a bit hard to say. I knew him so briefly." Phoebe stood on tiptoe to smell a honeysuckle growing on the other side of a pillar. As she leaned a little further out, she noticed a couple on the lawn beyond the lilac bed. "And I'd forgotten how…that's Charles and Isabela."

Emily stretched to see them also. "They seem to be enjoying each other's company." A slow smile spread across her face. "It is funny, don't you think? Not only did I hope to marry Hugh one day, but we also grew up expecting his sister to marry Charles. Now, she has eyes only for that Englishman you told us about, the one who resembles Bingley. I am glad Charles has found solace."

"And what of you and Hugh?"

"Nothing more than childish fantasies—and too few men of deep acquaintance. Do you remember asking me last summer how I might feel to be mistress of The Lilacs? I've given it much thought and don't think I could own someone, even if…"

Phoebe laid her hand on Emily's arm to stop her from finishing. "Here Hugh comes now to claim you. Aaron and I will meet you in the tent. I'm going around the house to avoid the crush."

Heading down the porch steps, she skirted the veranda, but as she looked back toward Charles and Isabela, she thudded straight into an unseen form. Hands quickly grasped her arms as she heard a low grumble.

"Miss Farrell, if you plow into me again, I'll think you are following me."

"Mr. Whitcomb." She badly wished to make some retort, but her respect for the Kikers would not allow it. "Whatever are you doing in the lilac trees?"

"The same as you, I gather—trying to navigate the crowd."

"Dinner is around back." She glanced at him sideways.

"Any sane person would avoid it presently. I prefer to snatch some…solitude."

"Well, then." She gathered up her skirts again. "I will leave you to it." For a moment, she thought he meant to detain her. He had loosened but not withdrawn his grip and his eyes were roaming her features.

"You have a mind of your own, don't you?"

"I hope so. I am sorry if that offends you."

"Quite the opposite, Miss Farrell. I've grown weary of women who adjust their thoughts and conduct to suit each man present. I find your wit refreshing."

"I am afraid you are confusing wit with a woeful lack of art." She pulled herself from his grasp and whisked away, refusing him a further opportunity to confound her, and spotted Aaron, Emily, and Hugh rounding the side of the house.

"Here you are," called Aaron. He stopped to wipe straw off his highly polished shoes. "Miss Nelson said you were in the garden, so we all thought we would meet you."

"It's still crowded around the tables," added Emily. "Are you alright? You appear flustered."

"It's that Mr. Whitcomb. He was…" Phoebe stopped, unable to put into words exactly what she meant. "I collided with him by the lilac bed."

Aaron creased his forehead. "He was not…impolite to you, was he?"

"No. It was just odd, him standing there by himself so snug into the trees that I did not see him until it was too late."

"And then what?"

"I ran into him, as he did to me in the Kikers' upstairs hall."

Hugh turned her way. "When was that?"

"A few days after you arrived home or perhaps the day after. The two of you and Mr. Pinder had escorted your sister to town. I thought Mr. Whitcomb was with your father, but he was in…I suppose it was his bedroom."

"Which room?"

"I can't say. I was pulling your mother's door shut when he knocked into me. She had sent me for her glasses. He appeared to have been walking while reading." As Phoebe looked up into Hugh's face, she saw his jaw tick, as if he were perturbed. "I meant no harm."

"It's not that. I am finding him…unpleasant."

"I think everyone is. This evening, he's made me a little afraid."

Aaron drew protectively close. "What did he do?"

"Many small things that would amount to nothing by themselves. I'm probably being silly and, frankly, unfair. I intentionally needled him while we danced and cannot be surprised that he reacted."

Emily chuckled. "I would like to have seen that. I've never known you to do any such thing."

"I overheard him implying my father was a bore."

"Ernest?" asked Aaron. "He is one of the most invigorating men I know."

"I agree, thank you. Hugh, please don't say anything to your mother. I don't want her to think I abuse your guests."

"More like a guest abusing you, but I won't mention it. We'd best get 'round to the back, though, lest she think we've gone missing."

# Chapter 19

AARON GUIDED PHOEBE through the dining tent up to the table where they selected delicacies from Mitilde's plentiful dishes. As Hugh ushered them through the crush to an open foursome of chairs, she felt pleased they were all eating together. Her friends would lessen the pressure to converse with Aaron, and Hugh had yet to tell her or Emily of his travels through Europe.

As he entertained them with a story about Italy, Phoebe noticed him shifting his attention and tilting his lips upward. Nothing appeared extraordinary as she followed his line of vision, but his expression switched from interested to satisfied. "What is it, Hugh?"

"Charles's attachment to my sister seems to be weakening." He leaned her over a tad so she could catch a glimpse.

"I see Charles but only the feather his dinner partner's wearing."

"It's the Nelsons' houseguest," answered Aaron, whose height offered an advantage.

"I am not surprised." Emily smiled. "We saw them together earlier in the garden." She inclined her head toward Phoebe who had grown unusually quiet. "Is everything all right?"

Phoebe pressed her lips together. Several of Isabela's inconsistencies were bubbling up in her thoughts, and she was having trouble whooshing them away.

"You might as well come out with it," advised Hugh. "It's easy to see something is troubling you."

"Occasionally Isabela lets information slip that belies her…condition."

Aaron cocked his head. "I thought Dr. Stillman had diagnosed it."

"He did, but what can he assert besides what she has reported?"

Hugh cleared his throat. "Emily, you have spent more time with her than any of us. What have you learned?"

"Precious little. She is so adept at redirecting conversations that become…difficult, I suspect she has had much practice. Beyond that, she is a perfectly pleasant person and so grateful for my grandparents' hospitality."

Aaron shifted his gaze to Phoebe. "Do you fear she may lead Charles on?"

"Not exactly, but she has stated emphatically she will not marry."

Hugh craned his neck to locate his sister. "Charles can take care of himself. I'm more worried for Clara. Wesley—Mr. Pinder—and she have raised so many eyebrows on the dance floor, Mother will be torn between scolding and congratulating her. They are dining together as we speak."

Phoebe saw him lower his brow sharply. "Who are you watching?"

"Whitcomb. He is with them, appearing bored, as usual, until a moment ago. He's staring at someone as if they were a specter."

Rising off her seat, Phoebe trailed Whitcomb's gaze. It landed on Isabela, who had turned as pale as the tent and clutched Charles's arm as if she might faint. "If you'll excuse me, I need to see what is wrong. Your mother will not want a scene."

While the musicians began laying bows to their instruments, she glanced back at the Englishmen. Clara and they had deserted their seats and several other guests were moving into them. When all three disappeared from her view, she could neither guess where they were going nor be bothered to find out. Isabela needed assistance.

Weaving through the crowd was easier than it had been earlier, though a good number of diners were still spread over the lawn in all directions. Once she was within an arm's length of the Nelsons, however, a row of low-backed chairs impeded her progress.

"Now?" Mama Nelson asked Isabela. When she appealed to her husband, he raised an eyebrow and began to shake his head.

"With your permission, sir," Charles cut in, "I'll find my little brother, and we'll drive Miss Isabela back to River Bend. I assume Sally will be there?"

Mary seemed relieved when the colonel assented. "If you are sure you don't mind, we'd appreciate it. Emily doesn't appear ready to leave."

Phoebe gained the merest glimpse of Isabela's face, but she could tell from the way she clung to Charles that she was either ill or severely plagued by nerves. Perhaps the evening *had* been too much for her. They slipped around the northern side of the house in the direction of the outbuildings where Charles normally stabled his horses.

Jeremiah was far more eager to spend time with Augie and the Kikers' animals than with their guests.

Returning to her friends, Phoebe accepted the glass of lemonade Aaron had fetched in her absence.

"Has everything sorted itself out?"

"Yes. Charles and Jeremiah are taking Isabela home."

"They can't be." Emily nodded toward the tent. "Jeremiah is over there with Mahala and Sarah."

Phoebe spotted Augie and her parents near them. "Then where did Charles and Isa…"

The dogs began raising such a ruckus, Hugh had to lean closer to hear what she was asking. "I'm sorry, Phoebe." He included Aaron and Emily in his gaze. "If you will all excuse me, I'd better go see what the trouble is. If they continue like that, they will disturb our guests."

"I'll come with you," offered Aaron, "if the ladies will excuse me."

"Of course." Phoebe watched Asa Kiker nodding gratefully as Hugh and Aaron passed him on the way to the stables. He was engrossed in a conversation with Judge Pennybacker, Governor McDowell, and Papa Nelson, and each appeared hesitant to end it.

As many of the other guests headed inside, Phoebe and Emily rose from their seats, and Megan broke away from Virginia and scampered over to them.

"Isn't he wonderful?"

"Hugh or Mr. Auger?" asked Emily.

The girl pulled a face that announced she thought the response ridiculous. "Mr. Pinder. After he danced with Virginia, he danced with *me*. Can you imagine? Me, Meg Simmons, dancing with nobility. Is he a duke or a baron?"

Phoebe shifted uncomfortably. "Where did you hear that? The Kikers decided they would keep the information to themselves."

"Lavinia let it slip to Ma. She is so excited for Clara."

"Then she may be disappointed. By the gentleman's request, Hugh has refused to say which one is titled."

"Pish-posh. Don't you think Clara has wheedled it out of him by now? Why else would her mother be so happy?"

"If behavior is any indication, Mr. Whitcomb is the more likely of the two."

"I'm sorry, Phoebe, I didn't catch all you were saying. Why don't they do something about those dogs?"

Phoebe had already been straining to pay attention to Megan, but now that her attention was called back to the barking, she noticed several more had begun yelping and howling. Where were Hugh and Aaron? Even as she asked herself, Augie ran up to Asa Kiker, grasping him by the coat while pointing and pulling him toward the outbuildings.

Mr. Kiker and the group who had been surrounding him rushed toward the stables. Phoebe scanned the remaining diners for Lavinia but surmised she must have gone inside. The musicians were playing a reel, and by the rhythm of feet on the polished wood floor, she suspected they were either oblivious to the disturbance or trying to ignore it. Thankful both Emily and Megan had been asked to dance, she trotted after the men, but by the time she caught up, the dogs were no longer in their pen.

"They went that way." Augie pointed Asa toward the woods. "You comin,' Papa Nelson?"

"Nah. Go ahead. I'd just slow them down." Spotting Phoebe, he caught her by the arm. "You'd better stay put. That forest will rip your skirt to pieces."

She knew he was right. "What are they chasing?"

"Don't know. Whatever it was certainly riled up the dogs. The stable boy told us Hugh was unable to restrain them. As soon as he opened the door to their pen, they squeezed past. He and your friend from Pennsylvania threw off their coats and tore out after them." He pointed to the growing pile of tailcoats tossed over the pen's half-wall.

Kitch's hands were shaking as he dusted each off and laid them out more neatly. "Colonel, you thinks I should fetch Missus Lavinia?"

"I'll take care of it." As he noticed perspiration beading the dark brow, he handed him a kerchief. "Try not to worry. It's most likely a bear or a mountain lion. Come on, Phoebe. Let's find Mrs. Kiker."

As she took the arm he extended to her and exited through the tall stable doors, he abruptly stopped. "That's the Simmonses' wagon. I thought Charles and Jeremiah were taking Isabela home. And where is their horse?"

"Jeremiah was with his mother a bit ago. Maybe Isabela is feeling better."

"Maybe so." He scratched his head. "We'll soon find out. You find her, and I'll look for Lavinia."

# Chapter 20

ONCE SHE PARTED from Papa Nelson, Phoebe searched both the dancers and watchers for Isabela to no avail. Charles, she guessed, might be playing cards, so she stuck her head into Mr. Kiker's study, but its only occupants were Emily's suitor, Graham Jamison, and a few others from Richmond she had not met.

Lavinia swished up behind her. "Where is everyone?"

Phoebe stared blankly for a moment. They were in a house jammed with people.

"I can't locate Asa, and I thought Hugh was with you. A few of our older guests are leaving and wanted to bid them goodnight."

"Colonel Nelson did not find you? Mr. Kiker and Hugh are following the hounds. The colonel suspects a bear or maybe a mountain lion wandered down to the barn."

"Again? We heard one a few evenings ago—a lion, not a bear—unsettling the cows." She spun her head toward the open rear doors and then back to Phoebe. "What is it? You're pinching your forehead together and giving me the same look Clara does when she isn't telling me everything."

"I think Kitch fears they are chasing a..."

"Out with it, Phoebe."

"He was acting agitated, as though they might be chasing...a runaway."

Curiosity, alarm, and anger raced across Lavinia's features, settling within a second into self-control. "Better not be one of ours! Those fool dogs. Where's Mitilde?"

"In the kitchen, I would suppose."

"Honey." Lavinia grasped Phoebe's hands and pulled her close. "I need you to do something for me that will require discretion. Count all the house slaves without letting them—or anyone—know what you are doing. Then, attend to our guests' needs as you would on any special occasion. And don't allow the musicians to take a break however tired they may grow."

While Lavinia swirled toward the foyer, Phoebe slipped through the kitchen, peeked out at the roasting pit and then at the back lawn and tent. All the house slaves were employed in one duty or another, except Jubal, Ruby's son. Skirting the perimeter of the room to check the lemonade and tea, she flitted her eyes everywhere she might to find him or Charles. John and Allison Wilson were both in the line of dancers, though not each other's partners, and she spotted William, his mother Mahala, and each of his sisters. Jeremiah appeared distinctly bored and was turning his head in each direction. She guessed he was looking for Augie.

"Jeremiah, why aren't you with my brother?"

"The stable hand sent me to retrieve Mr. Hugh's rifle and Augie to fetch your Pa, but when Ma saw what I was totin', she said I had to come inside."

"What did you do with the gun?"

"Handed it off to one of them gents who was heading out the door."

"Which 'gent'?"

Jeremiah shrugged. "I don't know. Maybe one of them Englishmen. Stranger to me."

No wonder Kitch was frightened, especially if he was aware the butler was missing; however, before she had a chance to fret, she spotted Jubal coming in from the veranda. Lavinia walked in front of him, looking particularly relieved.

"Are they all present, Phoebe?"

"Yes. I counted all but Jubal." She nodded toward him as he pushed through to the kitchen.

"Good." Lavinia let out a deep sigh. "It's none of ours. Kitch had already counted the field hands by the time Jubal and I found him. Lord O' Mercy, I pray it's that lion or…"

"Missus Lavinia!" Jubal strode up behind her, sounding out of breath. "Massa Asa's in the dining tent. Says you is to come quick."

Turning on her heels, Lavinia twirled toward the rear steps as the musicians commenced an allemande. Phoebe hurried after her. Out on the lawn, two men in livery were pulling the tent flaps closed but not before she caught a glimpse inside. The two Mr. Kikers and Aaron were lifting a dark-haired woman onto a cleared-off table.

"Land's sakes," exclaimed Lavinia, increasing her pace. "Who is it?"

Once they slipped through the slit, Phoebe clapped her hands to her mouth. "That's Isabela!"

"Surely, you are mistaken. She is as light-haired as Mahala."

"It is." Phoebe eyes roamed the fine features, coming to rest on the dark, well-shaped eyebrows. "I'm quite sure. Aaron, you danced with her. Wasn't this the gown she was wearing?"

As Mr. Auger nodded, Hugh retrieved a dirtied mass of golden curls and tossed it on the table. "A wig. Her attacker yanked it off. Look, you can see the lacerations…" He peeked up at his mother's face as he pointed to them and trailed off.

"Why," asked Phoebe, "is her head tilting that way?" She sucked in her breath as she spied a purplish-red mark spanning Isabela's neck where she had earlier worn a velvet ribbon.

Aaron took her by the shoulders and turned her away. "We'll know more when the doctor examines her. Mrs. Kiker, where's Whitcomb?"

"I…I don't know. He wasn't in the house. Why?"

Hugh, who answered for him. "He did this."

"Oh, mercy," moaned Lavinia. "You can't be serious."

"When I knelt to see if she was breathing, she whispered his name."

As both women glanced at Aaron, he nodded. "I was right behind Hugh and heard her clearly."

"And to think, he's been in our home for three weeks. Hugh, you've got to find him."

"The dogs," answered the governor, who had been standing in the background, listening, "are already chasing his scent. Has anyone seen my aide?"

"Mr. Jamison?" answered Phoebe. "He is playing cards."

"If you could ask him to join me here, young lady, and tell him to bring Judge Pennybacker also. He will need to open an investigation."

While Phoebe turned to carry out his orders, Lavinia caught her hand and nodded toward the house. "Tell the footmen to close and bolt those doors so that no one can come through them. It's bad enough that you have seen what he's done. It will not do for Emily or Mary to wander out here. And get Gary."

After carrying out their instructions, she peered through the opening between the dining room and parlor and spotted Colonel Nelson talking with the judge's wife.

"Mrs. Pennybacker, may I please borrow the Colonel?" When the woman smiled and nodded, Phoebe guided him from the room.

"Thank you for rescuing me. I didn't want to be rude to Mrs. Pennybacker, but I have yet to find Lavinia. Mary is asking me questions, and I can't forestall her much longer."

"I found her. She and Mr. Kiker need you in the tent, but you must go by way of the veranda." Phoebe ushered him through the foyer. "They wish to keep the rear way closed."

"Is something the matter?"

As he opened the front door, Lavinia darted up the porch steps. "Oh, Gary," she whispered. "I'm glad she found you. Go around back, please. Asa will explain." Once she and Phoebe were alone, she peeked surreptitiously in all directions. "How is everything inside?"

"No one appears to have noticed anything amiss. Did they find Whitcomb?"

"Not yet. I wish Matthew Bentley were here."

"I'm sure he'll come if you ask him."

"That's a good idea. I'll send Hugh tomorrow morning."

"What did Dr. Stillman say? Is she…dead?"

Lavinia put her hand to her throat and nodded.

"Where is Charles? He was supposed to be escorting her home."

“I have no idea. This is the first I’ve heard of it. We can talk about that later. I need to find a way to urge our guests to leave.”

“Are you sure? When we found Aaron’s grandmother, Mr. Bentley sequestered everyone in the home.”

“How in the world am I supposed to do that? We are using all but two of the guest rooms. Oh, Mr. Pinder! Everything is going so well between him and Clara. What is he going to think?”

# Chapter 21

ERNEST FARRELL SIGHED as he drove his family down The Pike. No one had spoken a word since they left The Lilacs, and his son appeared to be crying. "That poor young woman. Who would have done such a thing?"

"I don't care what they say," spouted Augie. "It wasn't Charles."

"Mahala Simmons's son?" asked Amelia. "Why?"

Her husband's lips drooped downward. "The poor boy has a knack for showing up at the wrong time."

"Whatever do you mean?"

"Last summer, he was their first suspect in his father's murder. You were still in Baltimore taking care of your mother."

"Poor Mahala. You haven't said *why* they suspect him."

"The Nelsons and a handful of others, including our daughter, heard him offer to escort Isabela home."

"Then why didn't he?"

"No one knows at this point. He appears to have fled."

"That's absurd. If he wanted to wring…" With a glimpse at her son's puffy eyes, she changed her wording. "I could understand if he were angry with Clara. The girl flaunted that English nobleman before him all evening."

"Hugh and Aaron are convinced it was Mr. Whitcomb," countered Phoebe. "When they found Isabela, she murmured his name."

Her mother gasped. "Isn't he the man I urged on you as a partner?"

"Amelia, we mustn't convict him until he's proven guilty. She may have said his name for any of several reasons."

"Such as?"

"She may have wanted him to convey key information, or she may have had feelings for him. We know little about her, and even Englishmen are entitled to a fair trial."

"I will grant that Mr. Whitcomb may not be guilty, but what possible motive could *Charles* have? They only met tonight."

"None of which I'm aware." He rubbed a hand over his face. "Ugh. How am I to preach in the morning?"

"You'll just have to do as you have always done—deliver the sermon you prepared. God knew perfectly well what would happen while you were planning it. Oh, poor Mary and Emily. They blame themselves for persuading her to go."

"Couldn't God have stopped him?" asked Augie.

"He could, but He gave us free will. What we do with it is up to us."

"I doubt the Kikers will come to church tomorrow," said Phoebe. "They are trying to sort out…"

"Papa—stop!" Augie leaned so far out of the wagon his sister grabbed him by his jacket. "What is *that*?"

Pastor Farrell steered the horse to the side of the road and pulled it to a halt. "I can't tell." He leaped from the buckboard and headed toward the dark form lying in the gully. Augie scrambled down after him, and when Amelia and Phoebe heard the reverend's sharp intake of breath, they followed.

"It's Charles!" cried Amelia, raising their lantern. "Whatever happened?"

"Can the three of you help me lift him into the box? We'll take him to Mahala. Where's Lucy?"

"In her basket, sound asleep."

"Augie, jump up and lower the tailboard."

The four strained with every ounce of strength they owned to lift him.

"Whew!" Augie wiped his sleeve across his forehead. "Why is he so heavy?"

"Dead weight," answered his father.

The boy's eyes grew as round as the full moon shining through the trees. "He's dead, too?"

"No son. He's breathing."

"Papa," asked Phoebe, "what do you suppose happened?"

"I reckon he fell from his horse."

Phoebe looked in every direction. "Then where is it?"

"This close to the Simmons place, it may have bolted for their barn." His expression turned grave. "Frankly, I hope I am mistaken. Fleeing is a sure sign of guilt."

Augie scrambled onto the buckboard. "He can't have ran, at least not for home. He's not stupid."

"Let's hope you are right, son. After we carry Charles inside the house, we'll check the Simmonses' barn. Does anyone know how William is bringing the family home? Judge Pennybacker detained their wagon."

"I do," answered Augie. "Mr. Kiker was packing them into his carriage while we were pulling away. Ruby's son said he'd drive them."

Despite the circumstances, that tidbit made Phoebe smile. Jubal would be able to spend time with his mother before heading north.

"Kitten, climb in and hold Charles's head still."

"Yes, sir." Once Phoebe adjusted her weight to keep him from rocking, she looked him over for signs of harm. He appeared perfectly fine, just asleep, much like Isabela had looked from afar. As her thoughts trailed to Isabela's bruises, her eyes wandered up his dinner coat and stopped. He was missing the button right over his heart. Such a loss was not surprising, especially as the coat's style announced it was slightly out of date, likely an old one belonging to his father.

Before the wagon crested Simmons Hill, the Farrells spotted lanterns coming down The Pike; and as they pulled to a stop close to the house, the Kikers' carriage turned into the lane.

Reverend Farrell hopped off the seat. "Augie, would you feel comfortable running over to the barn to look for the horse?"

The boy looked at the looming outbuildings, gray and ghostly in the moonlight. "May I wait for Jeremiah?"

"That's an even better idea, son. Here, Amelia, let me help you down. Mahala may need you, and Kitten, would you mind staying in the wagon with Lucy? That way, we won't need to wake her up."

As Phoebe assented, the carriage came to a stop, and the reverend had gripped the door before Jubal could jump from his box.

"Let me help you out, Mahala."

"Pastor Ernest, what are you doing here?"

"If you would, please come with me. You, too, William." He led them toward the church's wagon. "It's Charles. We found him not far from the lane."

"Charles? Here?" Mahala began wringing her hands. "Is he…"

"Just a fall. Seems to have knocked him out. Augie, why don't you and Jeremiah run along to check on the horse? William and I will help him into the house. Ladies, we may need you, too." He panned the Simmons sisters before climbing onto the wagon bed. "William, if you can take his feet, I'll grab his shoulder. Augh!!" The pastor cried out as a flailing fist hit his chin. "Stop, Charles! It's me."

"Huh? Reverend Farrell?"

"Yes, who did you think it was?"

Charles sat still for so long that Phoebe thought he had passed out again. "I can't rightly say. Where's Miss Isabela?"

"Charles," his mother began. "She's been…strangled."

"What!" He ran his hand through the thick dark hair atop his head. "How? Who?"

"We don't know, son," replied the reverend, "but first thing in the morning, you need to take yourself up to The Lilacs if you can manage it. Are you feeling all right?"

Charles shook himself. "My head hurts something awful, but other than that, I seem to be fine." He held up his hands to see how his fingers and arms were functioning.

"You and that Mr. Whitcomb are the primary suspects."

"Me? Why?"

"You appear to be the last person who saw her. What do you remember?"

"She was peering up at me with those big, vulnerable green eyes and…" He dropped his head into his hands for a moment. "She's dead? You're sure?"

"Very."

"I can hardly believe it."

"You were saying…"

"She was frantic, pleading for me to hurry, when someone hit me from behind."

The boys skidded to a halt. "Blaze's there!" Jeremiah interrupted. "Plenty lathered up."

The reverend glanced toward the barn. "Why don't you two rub her down while your brothers and I talk?" He waited until they were out of earshot. "Why did you ride off instead of raising an alarm?"

Charles rubbed the back of his head. "I don't remember a thing."

Phoebe flicked her eyes toward Virginia, recalling what she had said about Isabela's memory.

"William, you'd better fetch Dr. Stillman."

"He's still tending to…"

"I don't need a doctor, Pastor, but *I'll* go. I need to tell them what…"

Mahala rose to her full height. "Charles Edward Simmons, you'll do no such thing. Now get yourself into bed. William and you can ride up to the Kikers' tomorrow."

WHILE THE OTHERS took Charles into the house, Phoebe backed up against the buckboard's seat next to her little sister's basket. Lucy was still curled in a ball as if she were tucked into her bed in the nursery. When a door closed, she sat up, listening for Augie's scuffing tread, but the footfalls were so soft she was unsure she heard anything until Ruby's shadowy form scuttled toward the Kikers' carriage.

A larger figure grabbed the housekeeper in his arms, slung her around in a circle, and laughed into her hair as he set her down. "I'm going, Mama. Soon as this trouble passes over, I be free!"

"I'm so happy, Jubal, but I don't understand. 'Tilde said you was going by month's end. That's just a few days."

Phoebe began to scoot forward to make her presence known. She hated to disturb them, especially since their time together was precious and rare, but neither did she care to eavesdrop. Before she moved an inch, however, her ears perked up so suddenly, she pressed her hand over her mouth.

"Mr. Auger can't leave yet, Governor says so, least ways not 'til they finds who killed that woman."

Ruby cast a glance at the house. "Reverend Farrell says they's accusin' Charles, though I don't believe a word of it."

"They be questioning any man who's met her."

"Oh, mercy! What if they don't catch them the culprit or they settles on that Mr. Auger?"

"Now, Mama, don't go borrowing trouble. They got no reason to suspect him. It's just a delay, that's all. Missus Lavinia will see to it."

"All right, son, if you's sure. But Missus Lavinia ain't the Almighty. Only so much she can control." Ruby paused when she saw a light move closer to the parlor window. "I better go inside before they's missing me."

# Chapter 22

A PALL HUNG over the sparse congregation the next morning, even while they mouthed joyful praises. Closing her hymnal, Phoebe felt surprised to see Aaron Auger ascending the steps to the lectern. He smiled tentatively toward her and Emily as he flipped the Bible open to read the sermon text; and her friend's cheeks, still a bit blotchy from crying, began to warm.

"Beloved, think it not strange…"[xvi]

As he read about fiery trials, her mind wandered to last night's ordeal. It had been strange indeed, enmeshing her entire circle of acquaintances in its horror. While she wondered if Hugh had already wired Matthew Bentley, her thoughts leaped to the last time she had seen him and from there to Aaron's intentions. She felt a familiar kick in the gut but did not take time to trace its source. Her father was stepping into the pulpit.

Once he launched into the sad events of the previous evening, her attention wandered to the conversation she had overheard between Jubal and Ruby. It had confirmed the very discovery Ruby had urged her to forget: Aaron *was* the station master with whom Jubal would *ride the train,* though not literally. He must return home with the mounts Hugh and the Englishmen had borrowed, a perfect guise for the need of an extra hand.

She forced her mind back to her father's sermon. "Our lives," he was saying, "are not free from trouble simply because…"

A shift in Emily's posture drew her eyes once more to her friend and an idea vaguely planted during several incidents last week began to sprout.

"…He is not only our Creator and Savior but also the Keeper of our…"

Emily, she could tell, was also having trouble concentrating. Her gaze kept drifting toward the half pew near the front reserved for the morning's scripture reader and back to the gloved hands she neatly folded on her lap.

"…Lord bless you and bring you peace."

As the congregation responded with "Amen," Emily turned toward Phoebe. "I cannot believe Isabela is gone. She was with us only a…" She stopped as Aaron's shadow dimmed the light.

"Good afternoon, Miss Farrell, Miss Nelson."

Emily's color heightened, though she politely excused herself to offer Phoebe and him the little privacy they might grasp in the middle of a crowd.

"As you may have heard," he began, "considering your friend's …tragedy, Governor McDowell is insisting I remain beyond the month's end."

"What about your anthracite mine?"

"It will still be there when I return, and my Uncle Oliver is quite competent to see to any crisis that might arise."

Phoebe noticed Graham Jamison had attended service and looked as if he were watching them.

"You have spotted my guard. I had committed to your father to do the reading. Jamison's company was a necessary stipulation for me to come."

"They can't seriously be suggesting you had anything to do with…Isabela."

He flicked his eyes away. "It's merely a formality."

"Is it? You appear more concerned than you are admitting."

"It *will* be once Matthew Bentley arrives."

"The Kikers already sent for him?"

"Yes. He left before breakfast."

"And until then?"

"I am a northerner in a southern valley. If Jamison could pin Isabela's murder on me, he'd be delighted."

"Then I hope Matthew arrives swiftly."

They had moved along with a line of others to the church vestibule where Reverend Farrell shook his hand. "Mr. Auger thank you for coming. I would have understood had you not. Such a nasty business. Please join our family for Sunday dinner."

"I would gladly but can't." Aaron nodded toward Jamison. "He has agreed to give me some time to walk the church park with your daughter but nothing more."

"Then we will talk later. The man informed me before service that I am needed at The Lilacs."

Bidding the reverend farewell, Aaron offered Phoebe his arm and nodded a greeting to the Nelsons as they climbed into their carriage. "I enjoyed meeting your friends at River Bend earlier in the month and seeing each of them at the ball last evening. They must be suffering greatly from this shock."

His subdued tone, even as he expressed pleasure, reflected her feelings. "Emily looked as if she were taking the loss hard. Though she voiced a few doubts about Isabela's stories, the two had grown genuinely attached."

"You appear attached to Emily also."

"I've never had a closer friend. We were drawn to each other instantly."

"It is easy to see why you and Hugh are fond of her."

"Hugh?" Phoebe peered up at him. "What did he say?"

Aaron shook his head. "Nothing, though he claimed her for the first dance and for dinner."

"I am unsure that signifies anything beyond a preference for her over the Simmons sisters."

"Then I'm inclined to agree with his mother. Several Richmond gentlemen intended to leave their cards at River Bend this morning. She has a sweetness that is rare for one so lovely—very like you."

Phoebe blushed profusely. "You are generous with your comparisons. She is her grandmother in heart and features—and I can think of no higher praise. From the moment we stepped off the train, the Nelsons have extended themselves to our family, both by befriending my parents and becoming an extra set of grandparents to Augie and me."

"I overheard you address Mary as Mama Nelson and Augie called the colonel Papa. I've also met your aunt and uncle."

"My aunt and . . ." She cocked her head. "Oh—Allison and John Wilson."

"Yes, John was at The Lilacs this week discussing his rye crop with Asa, and he introduced me to his wife last evening. He told me his son lives out west—an envoy to the Indians or something like it."

"That would be Joshua. I have never met him. His godmother became a missionary of sorts who was so taken with a tribe that she married into them. He became interested through her letters. A consortium has published her story in a book entitled *A River too Deep* and her daughter's in a second volume. I'm sure Auntie Allison would lend both to you if you're interested."

"I will ask. They invited me to dinner before I leave for Pennsylvania and told me I may include a guest. Would you like to join me?"

Phoebe nearly stumbled. She had not expected to make their…friendship…public, particularly since her qualms had severely deepened. "Aaron, I have been thinking and praying frequently during these past weeks about our…possible future…."

He slid her a speculative glance. "From your tone, I suppose you are forming doubts. I am not entirely surprised. While we were eating dinner with Hugh and Emily I sensed a bit of…distance."

"I have been looking for a private chance to discuss them with you before either of us becomes further attached."

He stopped halfway down the slope to the river to offer her his full attention.

"If I wrote down your admirable qualities, the list would be lengthy. However, my mother instilled within me a good dose of practicality, and my father has taught me to listen to inner friction. I cannot ignore either."

"Which will you offer first, the practical or the inward?"

"Which do you prefer?"

"The practical. While I listen, I will steel myself for the other." As she glanced away, he steered her toward the bank. "Please speak plainly."

"I have been considering the helper God made for Adam and am convinced I wouldn't be a suitable one for you. Though I have learned much from Mrs. Kiker, I am not accustomed to entertaining the upper echelons of society. I would be lost. You saw me at your grandmother's dinner parties. I was polite at best and felt horribly awkward and out of place. You need a wife who has been steeped in the social graces and is accustomed to . . . diplomacy."

"You would learn, though since you are avoiding my eyes, I suspect there is something else, perhaps a bit more delicate."

Phoebe nodded. "My presence would thrust a wedge between you and your family. Neither Oliver nor Margaret will accept me as equals, and we've both seen the misery that caused your stepmother."[xvii]

"Her case is a little different. She had been a stage actress. Your father's occupations, current and former, are very respectable."

"And yet, you witnessed the way Oliver spoke to me."

"Yes." He nodded. "With antipathy, though as my wife, he would not dare. I would insist both he and Margaret treat you well or they would be unwelcomed to stay."

"I am confident you would, but that will cause me as much grief as relief. Oliver grew up there. The house connects him to his memories of his parents, and Margaret has called it home for nearly three decades. Besides, even if they held their tongues, I would see the censure in their eyes. Tension would underlie our daily interactions."

Aaron paused. "I cannot deny it and grant I haven't given it sufficient thought. What of the inner turmoil you cited?"

"You would be a generous and considerate husband, but the family business would naturally occupy your days. I would be counting the moments until you come home and spending my time making friends of the servants."

Aaron curved his lips. "*That*, I can easily imagine."

"You said I would learn what I presently lack." She began twisting the tail of a ribbon attached to her waist. "I do not wish to learn. The discussions in your grandmother's parlor felt as if they might never end. I care little about the latest fashions or who has or has not been invited to a particular party. I found myself searching for excuses to wander elsewhere—to find your grandmother's wrap or fetch things for Margaret."

"Would you have me marry someone more like *her*?"

"By no means." Phoebe smiled a bit mischievously while wrapping her ribbon tail around her finger. "I was thinking of a young woman whose loveliness you already admire—one who also, I am confident, holds you in high esteem."

Aaron lifted his eyebrows. "Miss Nelson?"

Phoebe nodded. "Neither your aunt nor uncle could object to her upbringing, and without that impediment, they would soon grow to love her. Can you conceive of anyone who would not?"

"I can't deny what I expressed not ten minutes ago, and I am sure she is all you say. However, I am not desperate to marry and want time to gain my bearings."

"Do not wait too long. All that Mrs. Kiker said to Hugh applies equally to you. You just told me several acquaintances from Richmond had planned to call on her if the evening had not turned out so horridly."

"What of Hugh? He is a friend. I would not try to steal her affections from him."

"I can't repeat any private conversations, but she has outgrown more than her pigtails."

# Chapter 23

ONCE REVEREND FARRELL finished saying grace, he passed his wife a bowl of peas. "Children, you are fortunate to have a mother who is also an excellent cook."

Amelia smiled with pleasure. "I enjoy cooking for my family. Phoebe, how was your walk with Mr. Auger? It's a shame he could not have joined us. Perhaps next Sunday."

Phoebe glanced from her mother to her father and then down at her plate. "Maybe, but as the whole family's guest. We decided we are best as friends."

Her father rested his fork. "You have?"

Phoebe nodded. "Are you…displeased?"

"Not at all, Kitten. The choice was always yours. I am just surprised. Unless he has made himself…odious…in some way, I assumed you'd consult your mother and I before deciding."

"Mama and I talked some last week, and I meant to ask your opinion, Papa, but when Aaron invited me to dinner this evening with the Wilsons, all my qualms poured out. You've always taught Augie and me to listen to internal turmoil, and isn't it better for Aaron to know how I feel sooner than later?"

Augie pushed his chair onto its rear legs. "Don't drag me into this. I like Mr. Auger."

"No one is faulting you, son," said Amelia. "You were saying, Phoebe…"

"I can't rid myself of the dread I feel each time I imagine married life with him. I'm seized with a need to escape."

"Well, Kitten." Her father rubbed his short beard. "Were it God's will to unite the two of you, I should think He'd give you a different sort of inclination. In my experience, the sense of foreboding you describe has been His way of nudging me off a course. Will you be able to maintain a friendship? Since he is managing your stipend from his grandmother, an amical relationship will offer an advantage to you both."

"Yes. I am sure, and I venture he will not long mourn the loss of me."

"I'll soon find out; that is, if he is not so disappointed that he avoids me. I'm headed over to The Lilacs after dessert. Don't sell yourself short, though. You have many unique qualities that keep me from believing you are so easily replaced."

"Why are you going to the Lilacs?"

"Judge Pennybacker wants to hear how we found Charles last night."

***

PHOEBE NOTICED A handful of unfamiliar carriages when she pulled into The Lilacs Monday morning and wondered how the Kikers were managing the extra house guests. As Mitilde's youngest son led Esmeralda into the stable, the front door banged.

"Mother is asking for you." Clara twisted her hands while she called from the veranda, but she waited until

Phoebe had reached her to continue. "They are detaining Charles."

"Oh no! I'd hoped the evidence my father gave yesterday might clear him."

"Phoebe, you've got to help."

"How?"

"I don't know. You are far more familiar with these sorts of proceedings than I am. Aaron told us you assisted the investigator when they found old Mrs. Auger."

"That's true, but what can I say of Charles? We didn't dance together all evening. Have they discovered any evidence against him—other than his disappearance?"

Clara closed her eyes and nodded. "Yes, though I'm not sure what. When Dr. Ridley examined…Isabela, he found something clutched in her hand."

"Oh, there you are, Phoebe." Lavinia stepped out of the house, the dark circles beneath her eyes declaring how little she had slept. "Judge Pennybacker has taken over Asa's study and his aide is occupying mine, so we will not be able to do our customary work today. I would have sent word for you to stay home, but they wish to see you directly. Would you like any coffee or breakfast? I can have Mitilde bring it to you there."

Phoebe flicked Clara a look of regret. "Yes ma'am. I will go to him immediately, and anything would be lovely if you think he will not mind."

"Whether he minds or not, you are my employee, and I will not have you going hungry. Besides, I would like you to see if I have left any letters out that we need to…attend to."

Phoebe nodded. She understood Lavinia exactly and, given the chance would carry off any incriminating correspondence however obliquely the messages in them were expressed. She also suspected sending in breakfast was Lavinia's way of asserting her ownership of the room. Winding through the foyer and left into the hallway, she stopped to lightly tap on the writing room's door.

"Come in." Behind her employer's desk sat the young man she and Hugh had been observing before the ball, the same aide that had engaged Emily in several dances and come to church with Aaron.

What her impressions of him were, beyond his pronounced sideburns and mustache, were harder for her to determine. She commended the marked attention he paid her friend while simultaneously viewing him as an intrusion. As he finished the notes he was writing, she spotted Lavinia's leather portfolio on the bookshelf.

"I am Graham Jamison. You are Miss Farrell, correct?"

"Yes." His eyes and hair, facial and otherwise, were a uniform mud-brown, and his features and build, while unremarkable, were pleasant. "Phoebe Farrell. I am Mrs. Kiker's secretary."

"I requested your presence regarding another capacity. Please, sit. Matthew Bentley has wired Judge Pennybacker and I concerning the help you offered him in solving two murders. The judge must return home today, but he has asked Governor McDowell to allow me to conduct a preliminary investigation."

"Mr. Bentley is not coming?"

"Not immediately, and as you are already aware, the quicker we can gather information, the more likely we are to solve this murder."

"How may I help you?"

"I would ask you to offer me the kinds of assistance you offered him. Be my ears and eyes. You are acquainted with the locals to a degree impossible for me at present and are more likely to notice any of them acting or saying anything out of the ordinary. I also wish to ask you the normal questions I am asking everyone who attended Saturday evening, which should give you ample cover for the time we spend together this morning."

"What would you like to know?"

"Do you recognize this?"

When she saw the button in Mr. Jamison's palm, her stomach dropped. The brass basket-weave on its fascia matched the ones she had examined on Charles's frock coat. Raising her eyes, she swallowed hard. He had seen her reaction; she was sure of it.

"Yes." She could do neither Clara nor Charles any good by dissembling. "Though it is a common enough design, Charles Simmons is missing a button of that sort from the coat he wore Saturday."

"And how would you know that, Miss Farrell?"

"I noticed its absence late Saturday night. While we drove him to his mother, my father charged me with holding Charles's head still. Papa has already told you how we came across him."

"I would still like you to describe what you remember. Your father was unaware of this detail and may have been of others."

While she was answering, Mitilde brought them both a pot of coffee and plates filled with eggs and bacon. "Missy Phoebe, Missus Lavina like you to join 'er on the veranda once you's through talkin' to Mr. Jamison."

"Yes, ma'am."

The man's brow knit together sharply. "Ma'am? Is that how you address a house-slave?"

Phoebe bit the inside of her mouth. Both Ruby and Mitilde had warned her about such mistakes. "I intended for her to give the response to my employer, sir. I trust Mitilde will convey my message."

"Take care, Miss Farrell. I am aware your family is from New Jersey, but it will not do for the Kikers or any other of your neighbors to presume you embrace…free-state tendencies." He licked off a bit of egg that had been dangling from his mustache.

"Thank you for your concern, sir. I will keep that in mind."

"What exactly is your relationship to Mr. Simmons?"

"Mine?" Phoebe sputtered. "Primarily, he is a fellow employee of The Lilacs."

"And more personally?"

"His family attends my father's church, and his sisters are among my greater circle of friends."

As he recorded her answers to his questions, she formed a few of her own. Did he sincerely desire her aid or was his request a ploy to gain her confidence? He had begun treating her as if she were shielding a guilty friend. Was she? Perhaps, she admitted to herself and considered the danger seriously. During a previous investigation, she had overlooked the guilty party for that very reason. She drew only one firm conclusion, which she tucked away for later use. The more suspicious he acted, the less inclined she was to speak freely.

# Chapter 24

WHEN PHOEBE RETURNED to the veranda, she found the Nelsons drinking coffee with her employer.

"What did Graham want to know?" asked Lavinia once everyone exchanged greetings.

"Nothing extraordinary. Emily, he wishes to speak with you next." She knew better than to mention the button. "Mrs. Kiker, I placed your portfolio in your bedroom. It contains several *invitations* you received last week."

When Emily hesitated, her grandmother patted her hand. "You have nothing to fear from Mr. Jamison. He had plenty of ladies to choose from at the ball, but you are the only one he expressly sought out."

"I did find him attentive."

Her grandfather's eyes twinkled. "Well, can you blame him?"

"Go ahead," urged Mrs. Nelson. "He will want to learn all you know about Isabela."

As Emily went into the house, Lavinia poured Phoebe a cup of coffee. "Mary thinks you and the other girls should discontinue your Saturday gatherings."

"I quite agree. We only started them for Isabela's sake. The poor girl. What could possess anyone to do such a thing?" Phoebe began fiddling with the trim on the lower edge of her bodice. "Do you think she may have been…running from something?"

"It has crossed our minds," answered the colonel. "What have you learned?"

"Nothing. However, during our discussions, she mentioned her feelings toward her younger brother and implied she had suffered a broken heart. These surely contradict the claim she lost her memory."

"Mary and I have wondered the same thing. During the last dinner your family ate with us, she depicted an estate she enjoyed by the water. If you recall, I assumed she was describing her home and encouraged her to continue, but she claimed she was speaking of River Bend."

"Yes, it rang rather false."

"I thought so, too," added Mary, "though to avoid embarrassment, I smoothed it over at the time. When you all left that evening, we wanted to ask, but we were afraid she'd conclude we wished to be rid of her."

Lavinia leaned over her cup. "I met her only once before Saturday evening, when you introduced us after church, but she struck me as a woman of wealth and good breeding."

"Gary and I came to the same conclusion. Her manners and clothes were not suited to a farmer's wife."

"How then," asked Lavinia, "did she end up collapsing on the parsonage doorstep?"

Phoebe shrugged. "Augie's guess may have been closer to the truth than we supposed—not that she'd been held in a dungeon, but that she'd escaped from someone."

Lavinia gasped. "Whitcomb! He might be her brother—or husband. We have only his word that he is a widower."

"That would explain why she whispered his name."

Colonel Nelson folded his hands in front of him. "Didn't you tell us he's from England? She spoke with a slight accent, but I wouldn't have guessed it was British. Closer to French."

Phoebe stopped toying with her trim. "I noticed that also—not so much an accent but a turn of phrase or an odd way she strung her sentences together."

Mary nodded in agreement. "Getting back to Augie's theory: didn't she say something about a cruel man during the girls' discussion of *Pride and Prejudice*? I was standing by in case Emily needed me."

"Yes." Phoebe plopped back against her wicker chair to retrace the conversation. "Virginia mentioned it the next day. 'The most handsome man she had known was also the cruelest.'"

Lavinia leaned forward as her daughter and Mr. Pinder came into view. They were strolling toward the lilac bed. "That hardly describes Mr. Whitcomb. Several more handsome men are presently dwelling beneath our roof.'"

"His features are nice enough," replied Mary. "What he lacks is charm."

Phoebe sat alert. "That was it! Not handsome—charming! She said he was the most *charming* man she knew."

"Well," replied Lavinia, "that rules Mr. Whitcomb right out."

As each sat silently for a moment, Clara emerged on Pinder's arm from the other side of the lilac bed. He was gazing at her tenderly, speaking in tones that sounded comforting.

Lavinia followed their progress across the drive. "He must be warm in that frockcoat this morning. We assured him he is welcome to relax his standards of dress—at least loosen his cravat—but I've never known anyone so fastidious. I hope he will not require such perfection of Clara."

Mary smiled in their direction. "Likely, he is anxious to make a good impression on his future in-laws. Are you having second thoughts?"

"Well…this woman's death has sobered my thinking. I would miss Clara if she moved to the next county; England is an ocean away. And what if she needed us? Titled or not, I hate to think of her in a foreign country at the mercy of strangers."

"He seems to adore her."

"Yes, but people aren't always what they seem. Even some of the most obvious aspects of appearance can be altered, let alone a person's character—your guest's hair color for instance. Who would have supposed it was so dark? Did you never see her without that wig?"

"Only on a few occasions, and on each she wore a turban."

Colonel Nelson pushed his coffee cup aside. "This 'cruel man' she mentioned—what reason do we have to connect him to her death? For all we know, he was part of her childhood…her father or a headmaster."

They all turned as the door opened. Emily walked over the threshold in front of Aaron, smiling over her shoulder in response to something he was saying. From the color in her cheeks, Phoebe guessed she was enjoying his proximity and apparently her grandfather agreed. He nudged his wife's arm.

Once clear of the door, Emily moved a polite distance away, reaching the table as Clara and her Englishman topped the steps.

"Please, all of you, join us." Lavinia gestured toward the group around the table. "Mitilde will soon be serving lunch, though I am afraid we may not be pleasant company."

Pinder pushed in Clara's chair and lingered over her protectively. "No one, especially a well-sheltered young woman such as Clara, would expect a childhood friend to commit such a ghastly crime. I can say little of him. We haven't spoken outside the performance of his duties, but I can imagine how shocked and shattered you each feel."

"I assume you are speaking of our foreman, Charles Simmons?"

Mr. Pinder nodded. "Though if we were living in the pages of one of Clara's novels, Whitcomb would be the more likely villain. I have not seen him since supper Saturday evening. Where are they holding him?"

"One of our vacant slave-cabins."

"And you, Mr. Auger? Has the magistrate's man cleared you for your journey?"

"Not yet."

"They suspect you, Aaron?" Lavinia looked dismayed. "For what possible reason?"

"When he searched my room early Sunday morning, he found tickets to Philadelphia, which the judge apparently deemed irregular."

"The train?" asked Phoebe. "I just assumed you would be returning on horseback."

Aaron flicked his eyes away. "The train will make up time lost while Jamison detains me."

Emily took the seat next to their hostess but kept her head tilted in Aaron's direction. "But how did you already know you would need them?"

Lavinia nudged her side beneath the table while the aide appeared at the door. "Why, there you are, Graham." She plastered on her most gracious smile. "It's about time you emerged from my tiny study. Come sit here." She pulled out the chair to her other side, but before she resumed her seat, she pressed a hand to her chest. "Oh, Aaron, I almost forgot. Hugh asked me to tell you he is in the office. Not Asa's study," she corrected when she noticed him glance at the house. "The distillery. I believe he wishes to show you the new piece Jubal's cousin just forged."

Mr. Jamison, who was parting his coattails to lower himself onto the cushion, stopped. "Mind if I go with you? I am curious to see how the distillery functions."

"Must you now?" Lavinia answered for Aaron. "You are welcome to tour our facilities whenever you wish, but Phoebe just recalled a conversation you will want to hear." She looked pointedly at her secretary. "She and all of our daughters took part in discussions held at River Bend for…for the murdered woman's benefit. Emily, you were the hostess. How often did you meet?"

"Twice, each on the consecutive Saturdays leading up to your ball."

"Phoebe mentioned a few of Isabela's interesting comments. Perhaps you, and Clara also, could help by adding your own recollections."

Mr. Jamison appeared torn between intrigue and irritation, and Emily was obviously taken by surprise. Phoebe, however, had caught the look that had passed between Aaron and Lavinia and guessed this was a ruse.

Neither of them wished Jamison to stumble into information that might be awkward—or perhaps deadly—to explain.

Taking Emily and Clara by the hand, Phoebe assumed what she hoped was an innocent expression. "Together, Mr. Jamison, the three of us may be able to recount Isabela's exact wording. Do you prefer we talk with you out here over lunch or in Mrs. Kiker's writing room?"

"Inside." His eyes followed Aaron, who had cleared the stairs and was heading toward the drive. "Thank you for the invitation, Mrs. Kiker. I will tour the distillery another time."

# Chapter 25

ONCE GRAHAM JAMISON had finished quizzing the three young women, he escorted them back onto the veranda. "Miss Nelson, may I call on your family this evening?"

"I will ask, but considering all that has happened, I'm not sure my grandparents will wish to have guests. We were attached to Isabela." As she turned her head toward the wicker table, she found only Lavinia.

"Sugar, Mary and Gary have already left. Since I do not need Miss Farrell to stay this afternoon, they thought the two of you might enjoy talking together on the ride home."

"That would be lovely. Phoebe, do you mind? It *is* out of your way."

Mr. Jamison cleared his throat. "If Miss Farrell finds it inconvenient, perhaps you would permit *me* to drive you home."

"I don't mind taking her at all." Phoebe looped her arm through her friend's. "We haven't had a chance to talk privately since the ball."

As the aide dipped his head, the two young women briefly curtsied. Swishing down the steps to the stable yard, they asked Kitch if he minded hitching up Esmeralda.

"What is it, Em?" Phoebe noticed her friend had grown noticeably quiet, though she could not decide if she were bothered or merely distracted. "Do you dislike the thought of receiving him?"

"I feel…awkward."

Kitch brought the wagon forward, and they situated themselves on the seat.

"Because of Isabela?"

"That certainly is a part of it. At the ball, Mr. Jamison seemed only a well-mannered man who was paying me attention. Since…later that night, everything I or anyone else says or does is tinged one way or another with her death. Besides, in the light of day and without evening clothes, he seems…less appealing."

"I feel similarly. Today, he was unnecessarily pugnacious, yet Saturday evening, I regarded him a man of impeccable taste. I saw him engineer an introduction to you."

"You were watching?"

"Hugh and I both were, but you were so deeply engaged in conversation, you never looked in our direction." Phoebe slid her a sidelong glance and found her blushing. "Are you uncomfortable with two suitors living beneath the same roof?"

Emily's face filled with confusion and something else harder to identify. It almost looked like guilt. "Is it true, what he told me?"

Phoebe dimpled. "That depends on who '*he*' is and what he said."

"Mr. Auger. He said the two of you are no longer courting."

Phoebe widened her smile. "It is, though I would not have characterized what we were doing that way. We were simply becoming better acquainted."

"Am I so obvious?"

"Only to someone who knows you well. I had meant Hugh, though I have noticed you and Mr. Auger enjoy each other's company."

"I do enjoy him." She clasped her hands firmly in her lap. "But if you mind, even a little, I will not encourage him."

"I cannot think of a more perfect match, and you have much to offer him that I do not."

Emily cocked her head.

"Mama is right. You grow more like your grandmother daily, and she is the most gracious woman I've ever known. I was watching her at the ball. Even though Mrs. Kiker was the hostess, your grandmother was constantly looking after other guests. She made certain newcomers gained introductions or found partners and, rather than talk about herself, she asked after others' welfare. I so frequently feel inept, I become lost in my own uncertainty. Combined with your reserve, you are perfectly fit for an industry captain's wife."

"I've always thought my reserve a flaw."

"Quite the opposite."

"How is it any different than what you expressed about yourself?"

"You think out your opinions before voicing them and consider well how you affect others."

"But you do the same. I cannot see any way in which you are lacking."

"That's because you don't hear my thoughts. Besides, you were born with something I can never obtain: a pedigree. Mr. Auger's family keenly insists on one."

"That has never mattered to me."

"Nor to Mr. Auger, but because it matters to his uncle and aunt, who live with him, you have already leaped an important hurdle."

"Are they so dreadful?"

Phoebe winced. She had not intended to influence Emily against them. "They won't be to you, and it's their flaw, not his. Who of us is without a tendency toward one sin or another? Perhaps if I were more enamored with him, facing theirs would not matter."

"I cannot imagine a man more wonderful. He is everything I dreamed Hugh might be and…oh, I don't even know how to describe him. You are laughing at me."

"I am not, honestly."

The hue of Emily's blush deepened. "I *am* letting my feelings run away. When he returns to Pennsylvania, I am unlikely to see him again."

"Mr. Jamison may keep him here long enough for you to become better acquainted."

"For his sake, I hope not. Still, I hope *so* for mine. Am I terrible to wish it?"

"Only if they detain him with serious suspicions."

"What suspicions can they have? He barely knew Isabela."

"No, but Hugh said your Mr. Jamison is a slave holder. If he has a nose for secrets, sniffing out Aaron's may lead down a long trail of others."

# Chapter 26

PHOEBE WISHED MATTHEW Bentley would hurry up and arrive. She was not clear what detained him, but it must be important. He would neither refuse the Kikers nor stay away with a murderer afoot. Deciding to be thankful for an unexpected day of leisure, she grabbed a book after breakfast and headed down the hill to the river.

She spread a quilt and lay beneath the willow she had long ago picked out as her favorite. While she gazed up through its thinning leaves, a warm late-season breeze blew across her cheeks, picking up strands of her hair and laying them across her lashes. She brushed them away, eager to immerse herself into the story, but she had read barely a chapter before her eyes began drooping. As she rested the novel on her chest and began drifting to sleep, a shadow darkened the dappled sunshine.

"Your father told me I might find you here."

Phoebe flung her eyes open. "Hugh!" Sitting up, she pulled her legs beneath her skirt. "Does your mother need me?"

"No. Jamison is still occupying her study. I was expecting you to be baking pies or some such."

"I offered, but since your mother gave me the day off, Mama wanted to do likewise. Where were you yesterday? I don't think I saw you once."

"With my father and then Charles. They've locked him and Richard Whitcomb in a couple of our vacant cabins."

"How is he?"

"Whitcomb? Spitting nails."

"I meant Charles."

"About as you'd expect. I'm not sure a jury could convict him on the evidence they have, but he has even less proof he is innocent. He still remembers nothing."

She wondered if Mr. Jamison had told the Kikers of the button. "I thought the onus was on the prosecutor to prove his guilt, not the other way around."

"It's supposed to work that way, and Judge Pennybacker is a fair man."

"How certain are you of Charles's innocence?"

She felt surprised when he paused to weigh his answer. "At one time, I'd have said, 'As sure as I am of my own,' but at the ball you mentioned something about my father's attitude toward him that got me thinking. You witnessed last summer how far Charles might go when possessed by a fit of temper—and you didn't know his father. Ed Simmons was the sort of man children and animals dodged when they saw him coming, and you know what they say: 'The apple does not fall far from the tree.'"

"He is from Mahala's tree too. I've never seen a man more remorseful than Charles was after he sobered. Did he drink heavily at the ball?"

Hugh ran a hand through his thick, dark hair. "Not that anyone noticed. Frankly, I've come to enlist your help. Although I can't deny my doubts, I can't believe he killed her either."

"Neither can I, nor understand why he would. I've read newspaper accounts of jealous husbands resorting to violence, but aren't those instances usually reserved for their wives?"

Hugh nodded. "Besides, from what Colonel Nelson told my father, Charles's desire to escort her home was an act of chivalry. Jamison has some crazy theory that she spurned his advances, but I'm not buying that. I've seen Charles tease a woman—like on the afternoon we stumbled upon you up to your neck in this river—but that's the extent of it."

Phoebe's thoughts leaped back to the old saying he had quoted. According to Lavinia, Ed Simmons had accosted women habitually. "What about Mr. Whitcomb?"

"I can't fathom why he'd strangle a stranger, but I admit I don't trust him."

"Do we *know* they were strangers? You described his change in demeanor when he looked Isabela's way during supper."

Rather than answer, Hugh began stroking his mustache.

"And," added Phoebe, "that's when she grew frantic to leave."

"You saw her?"

"Yes, though I can't guarantee it was Whitcomb who set her off. I never turned back to see who else was in her line of vision."

"I can tell you who. My sister, Pinder, and Mr. and Mrs. Yancy. Sari also. She was setting fresh food on the buffet while a flood of diners, including the governor and Jamison, were passing behind her." Hugh narrowed his eyes. "Earlier that evening, just before supper, you mentioned colliding with him."

"Yes, he had tucked himself between two lilac trees."

"Could he have been spying on her?"

"Possibly. I had assumed he was waiting for someone, though now that I say so, who? He danced with few partners …and she and Charles *were* close by. Emily and I had been watching them—not spying, of course—but while we were talking, they were in partial view."

"Did Charles act angry toward her, maybe raising his voice?"

"Not that I could tell. We heard nothing they said, but their tone was light, and both were laughing."

"Hmm…The sort of behavior that might rouse a surly former lover. Pardon my . . . indelicacy."

Phoebe smiled and shook her head. "Contrary to reputation, pastors' children are often exposed to life's ills. Earlier, you mentioned you don't trust Mr. Whitcomb. Why?"

Hugh resumed toying with his mustache. "Mostly my gut, though, in the past weeks I've also noted inconsistencies. While we were in New York, he expressed an avid interest in our whiskey production; yet he paid little attention to our distiller's demonstrations."

Phoebe crinkled her brow. "Does he need to understand the process to invest?"

"No, not strictly, unless he intends to start up a distillery of his own. However, a man usually desires to know exactly what his funds are backing."

"Has he? Decided to invest?"

"Not yet, nor has he bothered to examine the books, though Father has made them available. Pinder has poured over them as if his entire income depended on our profits."

"That does seem odd, though admittedly, I know nothing of business. I have qualms about him also. After he plowed into me in your upstairs hall, his behavior struck me odd. He dropped a recent wigmaker's bill, which would not be unusual except for the location of the shop. It was in a town he could not have visited since debarking the ship. You were with him."

"Where?"

"Baltimore."

"When I handed it to him, he grew. . .the word you used is as good as any: surly. At the time, I sloughed it off as his disposition, but Charles's brother, William, added to the mystery. He said one of your Englishmen dropped regularly into the shop asking if he had seen a 'raven-haired woman.'"

Hugh sat alert. "Your mystery woman wore a wig for a reason. Do you know which man it was?"

"I had assumed Mr. Pinder. We had met in town just before William told me the story. However, at the ball, he was unsure."

"Have you anything else to do today?"

She held up her novel. "Nothing demanding."

"Then let's swing by the Simmonses' home and ask him pointedly. If he's not there, we can ride up to the shop. I rode down in the phaeton."

"I can't without a chaperone."

"That's right. I'm so used to ferrying Clara, I hadn't thought."

"Let's ask…"

"Augie!"

# Chapter 27

AUGIE GRINNED FROM ear to ear as he ran to Hugh's phaeton. Except for a brief greeting while he passed through The Lilacs' receiving line, he had not seen Hugh since his departure for Europe.

"I thought you'd never come to visit! You've been back for nearly a month."

"Sorry, Squirt. I've been occupied with guests I brought to The Lilacs."

"Are they gone?"

"They planned to leave yesterday morning, but this. . . horrible business has detained them."

The boy's countenance fell.

"You seem to be taking it hard."

"Yeah." He rubbed a small nick on his knuckle. "I never got to show her the good fishing spots at River Bend."

As Phoebe opened her mouth to reason away his feelings, Hugh gave her a sharp shake of the head. "After we return your sister to the parsonage, will you show them to me? Maybe the colonel will join us."

Augie's eyes lit up. "Could we?"

"I don't see why not. How's that pup of yours?"

"I'll tell you on the way."

During the short ride to the Simmonses' farm, Augie told Hugh about Sparkles' latest adventures: the ruckus he made while treeing a racoon and the aftermath of cornering a skunk. "You should've seen Mama when she smelled. . ."

He trailed off as they spotted William emerging with a bucket from the barn. Jeremiah was lugging a pail toward some chickens when Hugh pulled to a halt by the horse pen. "Morning, William! Doing Charles's chores?"

"Some. I'd forgotten how much I hate farming."

Jeremiah squinted at his brother and pulled a face.

"Morning, Phoebe." William tipped his straw hat. "Hugh, has Judge Pennybacker given y'all any idea when Charles might be released?"

"None. We've come in hope you can clear up a few points."

Augie nudged Hugh's elbow and pointed to the contents of the younger brother's pail. "May I help Jeremiah feed the chickens?"

"Sure, Squirt, but don't be long. Fishing takes time."

As the boy scrambled down, William rested a hand on the phaeton. "What do you need cleared up?"

"For one thing, did Charles know the Nelsons' mystery guest before Saturday evening?"

"I reckon not, but I can't be certain. Yancy keeps me busy. 'Course, all that may be changing soon." He rubbed the back of his neck and flicked his eyes toward the house. "Charles never talked about any woman…except your sister."

"What did he say?"

William shook his head. "Nothing you don't already know. What else?"

"Phoebe related a conversation you had with one of my English guests, but she is unclear about whether it was Pinder or Whitcomb."

"Gabriel something or another."

Hugh cocked his head and glanced at Phoebe. "That's not either of their names."

William shrugged. "That's what Ginny and Meg call him. Fancy way of speaking and manners."

Jeremiah, who had scampered back with Augie after flinging the chicken feed, yanked on his brother's shirt. "No, William. It wasn't *him*." He tipped his head toward Phoebe. "It was the brown-haired gentleman who fancies Augie's sister."

"Don't interrupt. You don't know what we're talking about."

"Do too! The man in the barn."

Hugh knit his brow so sharply, his whole forehead crumpled. "What man, Jeremiah? Can you describe him?"

"'Bout the size of Charles."

"What color were his eyes?"

"Like his hair, I think."

"And he had an English accent?"

"I don't know. He just talked funny—sorta like the Farrells."

"Did you hear what he said?"

"Think," urged his brother. "Charles's life might depend on it."

"Didn't catch nothin.' He was talkin' too low."

"Well, *who* was he talking *to*?"

"I don't *know*! He was hidin' in the dark."

"Could you say if it was a man or a woman?"

"I already told you." Tears glistened in the boy's eyes. "I don't know!"

Hugh cast William a cautioning glance. "It's all right, Jeremiah. Is there anything else you remember about the man you did see? Did he have scars or facial hair?"

The boy reflected for a moment. "His hands. They was smooth, not like Charles's or yours, more like Judge Pennybacker's."

"When did you see the judge?"

"B'fore your pa piled us into your carriage. Ma made me tell."

Phoebe's chest felt so hollow she feared she might faint. She could not blame Mahala; she was protecting her son, but she now understood why Jamison had been eyeing Aaron.

"What, exactly," asked Hugh, "did you tell him?"

Jeremiah swiveled his head toward Augie. "We were in the dog pen, before supper, when he snuck in and crept toward the back."

"You saw him too, Squirt?"

"It wasn't like that." Listening to Jeremiah, Augie had grown pale. "He was just talking to . . . to. . . someone."

Phoebe leaned half-over Hugh to get a better view of her brother. "Why didn't you say something?"

"I don't know. I didn't think anything of it. Mr. Auger wouldn't hurt anyone. Besides. . ."

"Besides what?"

"Oh, nothing." Augie nudged the gravel with his shoe. "You wouldn't understand."

"Of course, I can't if you don't tell me. . ."

Hugh gave Phoebe's hand a quick squeeze and jutted his chin at the Simmonses' front path. Mahala and Virginia were walking toward them. "Don't worry, Squirt. We'll get it all sorted out."

"Good afternoon, Hugh, Phoebe." Mahala ambled up to the driver's side of the phaeton as Virginia slid around to the passengers'. "William, you should have told us we have company. Please, come in."

Even as Mahala attempted a warm welcome, her face held clear signs of strain.

"Yes." William reddened. "Where are my manners?"

While Hugh accepted, Virginia leaned toward Phoebe. "Do you think we might take a walk through the pasture?"

Phoebe looked at Hugh, who nodded. "I'd enjoy that."

As Virginia led her through the grassy field, she began wringing her hands. "Do you remember your apology in the church yard a few weeks back?"

"Yes."

"I'm the one who should have said I was sorry. Charles's detention has cast our conversation about the Nelsons' mystery guest in a different light. It pains me to learn how people are speculating about him. And that poor woman. I can hardly believe she is.... I don't even want to say the word. I was petty and rude to you at River Bend."

As Phoebe started to respond, Virginia shook her head.

"Please, don't stop me. I want to get it all out at once. You hadn't intended to hurt me. You were trying to prevent me from causing Isabela pain. I *meant* to embarrass you. Can you forgive me?"

"Of course." Phoebe touched Virginia's arm and then folded her into an embrace.

"I'm a horrid person and don't deserve your friendship."

"Ginny, you deserve mine as much as I deserve yours."

"No, I don't. I'm jealous of your job with the Kikers and...and of how everybody likes you. You are always so kind; I can't keep my horrid thoughts from flying out of my mouth."

Phoebe stroked her friend's ginger-tinged hair. "I know that struggle well, at least when I'm not feeling timid. I used to try so hard to be genuinely good, but I just couldn't, especially toward Augie. It was so frustrating."

Virginia raised her head to look Phoebe in the eye. "What did you do?"

"I gave up trying."

"But…" Virginia dropped her arms and took a step backward. "You're a pastor's daughter."

Phoebe frowned. "That only makes my faults more obvious. People tell my parents whenever they think Augie or I are out of line. Worse yet, we read the Bible together every morning, and I just couldn't live up to the standards Jesus set—any of them—and often didn't want to."

"But you seem so genuinely…good. What happened?"

"I fell on His mercy—very like Augie did with Mrs. Kiker during last years' Lilac Ball."

Virginia shook her head. "We weren't there…because of Pa."

"Oh, that's right. I should have remembered. I'm sorry."

"It was a long time ago. What did Augie do?"

"He backed into their large silver bowl, slinging punch all over his shirt and the rug. Then he used the Kikers' finest napkins to mop it up."

Virginia winced. "Poor Augie! He must have felt mortified."

"We all did. Papa offered to pay for the damages, though I now realize that would have been impossible. Their rug came all the way from China."

"What did Mrs. Kiker do?"

"She was very gracious. When I began to scold him, she stopped me."

"What did your Ma say?"

"She was still in Baltimore with my grandmother. Mrs. Kiker sent Augie to the kitchen. All his efforts—however sincere—were fruitless, and even if he were perfectly careful during the rest of the evening, that wouldn't have fix the mess he'd already made. He needed someone who could get the stains out."

"Ah." Virginia's eyes showed dawning awareness. "I was wondering how you were connecting my question to this story. You were unable to remove your stains."

Phoebe nodded. "I needed Jesus to do it. He gave me a new heart."

"Is that what your Pa means? He is constantly saying, 'Changed hearts change habits.'"

"Yes, and I can *see*—or maybe I should say *feel*—the difference. I no longer need to *force* myself to 'be good.' Pleasing Jesus is what my new heart *wants*."

# Chapter 28

WHEN THE TWO girls saw Hugh and Augie waiting, they agreed to talk later and gave each other a final hug.

"Please, come over on Saturday," Phoebe requested. "Mrs. Nelson suggested we suspend our book club in light of…what's happened."

"If Ma will let me use the wagon."

"See you then."

As Hugh lifted Phoebe into his phaeton, he noticed she was dimpling. "Good news? We could all use some right now."

"Just the end to a previous conversation."

"Then I assume it ended well, but I won't pry."

"It did and thank you."

By then, they had reached the end of Simmons Lane. "Where to?"

"You might as well take us home. We've already talked to William."

"But Hugh promised we'd go fishing with Papa Nelson!"

"We will—after we drop your sister off."

Phoebe worried the button on her glove. "Augie, are you certain the man you and Jeremiah saw was Aaron Auger?"

"No doubt at all."

While he bobbed his head emphatically, Hugh caught Phoebe's eye. "There isn't any point in us bringing that up to Jamison."

"Do you think Aaron was making arrangements with…" She glanced at her brother and trailed off. He was avidly listening.

"Just say it," spat Augie. "Nobody can hear us. Besides, I'm not blind. I saw Jubal with my own two eyes."

Hugh pulled the phaeton off onto the side of the road. "You'd better keep that between the three of us, Squirt, do you understand?"

Phoebe had never heard him sound so stern.

"Yes, sir."

"Telling someone else will only raise questions that are best left unasked."

"And that includes Mama and Papa," his sister cautioned, "and every other living human on the face of this earth."

"Papa already knows. What do you think he was doing Sunday night?"

"I don't know what you are talking about." She saw a vein near Hugh's temple had begun to throb. "But you'd better take the advice a wise woman recently gave me: 'forget whatever it is you think you know.'"

"You live with me, don't you? Have you heard me say one word?"

"Yes," cut in Hugh, his voice firm. "Just now you told her an earful. Have you ever wondered what happened to the last pastor and his family?"

The boy shook his head.

"He barely escaped a lynching. When the slave catchers discovered what he was doing, his whole family had to flee, and no one has heard anything but rumors about them since."

As Augie's eyes looked like they were about to pop, Hugh leaned forward and peered intently into them. "Your observations—which I'm *not* confirming—could prove deadly to your father. Sisters are often pests, but yours is right. Don't utter one more word about your suspicions—not to Phoebe, not to me, not to your father, or to anyone else you think might share them. Do you understand?"

"Yes, sir."

As they turned up the hill to the parsonage, Ernest and Amelia waved eagerly. They were walking with Lucy to the church's wagon.

"We were coming to find you," said the pastor. "Jubal just left. We're all wanted at The Lilacs. Now don't look so worried. It's joyous news, though I've been sworn to secrecy about its nature. Jubal's on his way to the Nelsons to fetch them and Mr...." He peered at his daughter and hesitated.

"Auger?" Phoebe couldn't help dimpling, though her mother shot her a sympathetic smile. "What about the Simmonses?"

"He's swinging by their place on the way back, though Mahala may not be in the mood to accept an invitation since her son's locked up on their property. I'm sorry, Hugh. We're all aware neither you nor your family is at fault."

Hugh sat back for a moment. "I hope she and the whole family come. A visit from them would do Charles good."

***

PHOEBE WAS NOT sure what to expect as she crossed The Lilacs' threshold, but the voices wafting from inside sounded far from gloomy.

"Why there you are, son!" When Lavinia had heard Hugh's voice, she had rushed to greet him. "And Augie and Phoebe. I'm so happy you could join us. Where are your parents?"

"They're coming up the steps."

"Mother, what's this all about?"

Lavinia laid a hand on Hugh's arm. "You will see. Don't be impatient, or if you just can't wait, go ask your sister." She nodded toward Clara, who looked stunning if not joyous in a peacock blue gown. Pinder, though flushing bashfully, was equally elegantly outfitted. "Oh, here are Amelia and Ernest. Come in! How huge Lucy's eyes appear in her blue bonnet!"

When Phoebe rounded the corner into the dining room, her heart lurched. She locked eyes with a man by the windows. He was standing as still as the stone gargoyle Aaron's Uncle Oliver had once called him and staring at her just as fixedly. As his filled with warmth, she dimpled, but she did not have the temerity to hold his gaze. Instead, she panned the room for his employer, Matthew Bentley.

Without her knowing how he managed it—the room was rapidly filling, and he had been sitting at its back—he slipped up beside her so silently, she startled. "Mr. Dyer!"

"Miss Farrell."

"Where is Mr. Bentley?"

"He is awaiting the birth of his first child, so he sent me in his stead. Mr. Jamison told me to watch out for you."

Phoebe arched a brow. "In what way?"

"He used the word 'nuisance.'"

"Why, sir!" She imitated Lavinia's deepest southern drawl, pressing her hand to her chest as her cheeks began twitching. "I am shocked!"

The sparkle in his eye proclaimed he caught her meaning perfectly.

She searched the room. "Is Mr. Jamison here?"

"No, but I see someone I hadn't expected." Mr. Dyer tilted his head toward the door. "The younger Mr. Auger."

When she turned, she saw Aaron coming in behind Emily, appearing every bit as absorbed by her as she was by him. "He is an old friend of the Kikers. He accompanied Hugh here from Pennsylvania."

"The young man who walked down the hall with you?"

"Yes. He is the Kikers' son." At once, Phoebe stopped smiling. "What is Mr. Whitcomb doing here?" He had entered through the double doors to the parlor.

"I haven't sufficient evidence to hold him. Besides, he was squawking about contacting his ambassador. The Judge is certain Charles Simmons is our man. By the angst in your face, I'm guessing you disagree. In fact, now that I think of it, Jamison accused you of shielding him."

"I merely mentioned his prime evidence was of a common type and that Charles hadn't any motive."

The corners of Mr. Dyer's lips rose almost imperceptibly.

When Phoebe saw Mama aiming her father's attention in their direction, her smile faltered. She did not know why. Neither she nor Mr. Dyer needed to hide their acquaintance, yet she felt it unexpectedly important to keep them from meeting. The idea was ridiculous. Mr. Dyer would surely quiz her father if not both her parents about their observations at the ball, but she did not want to be the one to introduce them.

"I should help my mother with my little sister." She gestured toward her family. "Lucy is typically napping at this time and may grow fussy."

The glimpse he took of Phoebe was nearly as slight as his smile, yet she felt certain he was amused. "I understand you will be here in the morning. Can you find the time to make yourself a 'nuisance' to *me*?"

She smiled as he inclined his head. "I will do my best."

# Chapter 29

ASA KIKER CLINKED a spoon against the whiskey glass he was holding. "If I could have everyone's attention, please, I would like to tell you why we've gathered you here this evening. As you all see, our Clara has grown into a young woman who rivals the beauty and grace of her mother. Although parting with her will not be easy, the Earl of Dunham, whom we introduced to you as Wesley Pinder, has won her heart and asked for her hand. How can we refuse our consent? Please join me in raising a glass in their honor."

For several minutes, he remained silent while the gathering of friends clapped or called out congratulations and best wishes.

"You may wonder at our haste. My soon-to-be-son has an estate of his own to run in Surrey and made unalterable plans to set sail on Monday, next. This was all before he met our lovely Clara; and since her mother and I are unable to make the voyage before the spring, he has convinced us she would be far better served by sailing as his wife than later with a chaperone. So—you, our dearest friends—are invited to the church for their wedding this Saturday."

As all present broke into another round of well-wishing, Virginia tossed Phoebe a look of regret that they must cancel their plans and made her way across the room. "Can you believe it—my closest childhood playmate marrying an earl? What must we call her?"

"I'm not sure. Do you know Aunt Allison?"

"Countess, though we will not have much opportunity. I'd assumed, from his imperious manner, Mr. Whitcomb was the secret aristocrat."

Uncle John grinned. "That would have placed the Kikers in a pickle. They've had him locked up since the ball. The line is shrinking; let's go congratulate them." He placed his hand on the small of Allison's back. "Ernest, are you performing the ceremony?"

"I am, and I'll be announcing the couple to the congregation the next morning."

"Kitten," Phoebe's mother began. "Who is that young man by the windows with whom you were speaking earlier? You appeared to know him."

"His name is Alan Dyer. Mr. Bentley's wife Tandy is in her confinement, so he sent his assistant in his stead."

"Dyer? Isn't that…" As she noticed her daughter's change in color, she decided not to finish.

"Isn't he what, Amelia?" The reverend peered at his wife over their toddler's bonnet. "You and Phoebe are forever leaving off the ends of your sentences."

"Oh, nothing, dear. I was simply recalling where I'd heard his name. Matthew told us he had clever ways of discovering poisons."

"Ah, yes. The man with the rats."

Auntie Allison laughed. "You make him sound dreadful."

"Speaking of dreadful," Uncle John grew serious. "Are they any closer to catching that woman's murderer? Graham Jamison left about an hour ago."

What they concluded Phoebe did not hear. Aaron Auger, who had joined them, claimed her attention.

"I saw you talking with Bentley's assistant."

"I was. When do you think he may strike you from his suspect list?"

"That remains to be seen. Lavinia told me his train arrived this morning."

"May we speak outside for a moment?"

"Of course."

Once they passed through a side door, he leaned against the railing and stared up at the stars. "What a lovely night—not so cold as the last time we were alone on a veranda."

"I remember well." Her smile was wistful. "The snow blanketed your grandmother's lawn.

"Did you want to escape from the warmth inside or did you desire to talk with me? I could not help seeing your head turn as Emily and I entered together." His eyes assessed her caringly. "Do you mind? I mean, so soon after we decided we were better as friends. It was you, after all, who threw me over."

Phoebe's countenance dimmed. "Please do not take it that way. Have I hurt you?"

"A slight wound to my pride, but I understand your reasons. If I am to be frank, I'm ashamed I never considered them. I was aware you witnessed my aunt and uncle's snobbery but never gave thought to how miserable they might make your life."

Phoebe dipped her head. "A man who freely admits a failing is surely rare. You almost make me regret my decision. To answer your question, though, I am glad the two of you are getting better acquainted. Have you mentioned your interest to Hugh?"

"Not yet. I wanted first to see if I had anything to tell him." He broke his eyes away from hers, as if considering his next statement. "I've noticed he pays you a copious amount of attention."

"Not in the ways you might imagine, but you've reminded me why I asked you to come out here. I must warn you: Jeremiah and my brother heard you speaking with…someone…in the barn. Jeremiah didn't see who."

"Did Augie?"

Phoebe nodded. "He will say nothing."

"Thank you for warning me. Shall I infer you think me innocent of Isabela's murder?"

"I never doubted you."

Aaron's brown eyes warmed. "Whomever either of us marry, I hope our lives will always stay connected and you will consider me among your friends."

"Always, and I hope you will likewise."

As the door opened, they turned their heads.

"There you are, Kitten. The congratulatory line has shrunk, so your mother and I wish to deliver our well-wishes so we can take our leave. Do you mind, Aaron, if I steal her?"

"No, sir. Will you be in your office at the church tomorrow?"

"I intend to be."

"Then, I will bid you both a goodnight."

Phoebe smiled up at him. "I wish you success, Mr. Auger, in all your pursuits."

"You also, Miss Farrell, and remember what I said."

"I will."

When her father opened the door, the three Nelsons streamed through it, but before Phoebe had a chance to speak with them, Mr. Auger was offering Emily his arm. Mama Nelson shot her a glance at once questioning and sympathetic which Phoebe answered by dimpling happily.

As Phoebe rounded the doorframe to the parlor, she caught a glimpse of the bride-to-be. Clara's lips had slid downward, as if she were weary of keeping them pinned in place, until William Simmons extended his hand. She *had* been smiling continually, reasoned Phoebe, enough to make anyone's cheeks ache.

Her parents stepped into line after Mahala and her daughters and soon reached their host and hostess. "Well, Asa," began her father, "you've not only gained a son but a business partner."

"Indeed, I have, Ernest."

Phoebe watched Hugh's eyebrows pull together infinitesimally. She was certain his sister's engagement was as new to him as it was to everyone, and he had been fully occupied ever since Asa's toast. Perhaps her father's comment gave rise to questions he had not yet had time to consider.

"They are certainly an attractive couple."

"Ah, Lavinia," added Amelia, "We are so happy for you all. I only wish his home was not an ocean away. That will be hard for you."

"It surely will, but Clara's happiness is what matters to us most." Lavinia turned from them to Phoebe.

"Congratulations, Mrs. Kiker. Shall I come to work tomorrow?"

"Please do." Lavinia smiled. "Now that I have my writing room back, we have much to do. Mr. Dyer appears to roam as he works. Besides luncheon, we hardly saw him in one place for ten minutes. Feel free to delay your arrival. Between this horrid business and Lord Dunham's sudden proposal, I suspect we will all sleep in."

# Chapter 30

WHEN AMELIA HEARD knocking at the parsonage door, she tossed her daughter a look of pleading. She had tied Lucy into a chair and was trying to feed her cornmeal gruel. "Who could that be?"

"I'll get it, Mama." Untying her apron, Phoebe slipped it off as she hurried into the foyer, flung it on a coat hook, and unfastened the bolt. "Mr. Dyer." The humor in his eyes made her feel self-conscious. "What's wrong?"

"I thought powdered wigs were out of fashion."

Ducking in front of a small hanging mirror, her cheeks flamed. She must have swiped her face with flour while smoothing back her hair.

"Allow me." He swept his thumb across her forehead. "Personally, though, I thought the streaks a nice addition."

Unsure how to take his remark, she continued as if he had not made it. "I am surprised to see you so early."

"I decided I'd better come to you. Concealing the extent of your help is to my advantage. The younger Mr. Kiker tells me there is a bench in the park with a nice view."

"Yes, just go around to the back." She reached for her bonnet but stopped as he pointedly looked down at her feet.

Ducking her slippers behind the door, she leaned her shoulder against it. "I will be with you shortly. I need to change."

"I hope you never will."

She glanced at him blankly, but as he replied only with that enigmatic tilt of the lips, she leaned out the door and pointed to the garden path. "The bench sits atop the rise. You cannot help but see it."

"I will wait for you there."

"Kitten," called her mother as she shut the door, "who was that?"

"Mr. Bentley's assistant. "He wishes to ask me some questions."

Mama came into the foyer, wiping her hands with her apron as Phoebe headed up the stairs.

"He must be an early riser. I will make him a cup of coffee."

"I'm sure he'd like that." Phoebe had reached the upper landing. "He must have set out before dawn. Oh, Mama, I forgot my apron. It's there on the hook."

Amelia smiled. "I suspect your mind was elsewhere. I'll put it with the laundry."

Phoebe turned on her heel without answering, and once in her room, cast aside the faded house-frock she was wearing. Opening her wardrobe, she pushed aside her drabber choices and settled on a serviceable but attractive gown Clara had given her last spring. She blushed anew as she donned her stockings, the memory of Mr. Dyer's fingers on her forehead still fresh, and took care to brush out all traces of flour before she refastened her hair. "You are a silly goose." She peered into the mirror as she finger-curled a tendril near each temple and another on each side of her neck. “He is here to only conduct an investigation.”

Swirling into the hall, she stuck her bedroom key in its hole and turned the lock.

“Hey, watch it!” snarled Augie as she slipped it into her pocket. “You nearly knocked me over.”

“Well, I didn’t. What are you doing up here anyway? You are supposed to be in the parlor completing your arithmetic.”

“Why should I tell you? What did you do to your hair? You look like you are going to a… Hey, is Hugh coming over again?”

“Not that I know of.” She swished toward the stairs and scampered down them before he could ask another question.

“Here, Kitten.” Her mother handed her a pewter mug. “I’ve not seen you wear your hair quite like that before. It is very becoming.”

Phoebe took the mug in such haste she nearly sloshed out its contents. “Thank you, Mama.” She did not want to answer her mother’s questions any more than she wished to reply to Augie’s. Taking the route through the kitchen, she deftly avoided Lucy’s sticky little fingers. “Not now, dumpling. I have hot coffee in my hands.” Once outside, she took a moment to smooth her skirt and push back her shoulders.

“Don’t rush on my account.” Mr. Dyer spoke as if he had eyes in the back of his head. “You will spill my coffee.” No sooner did Phoebe wonder how he knew what she was carrying than he answered her question. “I can smell it.”

“Would you like anything for breakfast? I’m sure I can find something.”

"Thank you. Just coffee. Is this the Shenandoah?" He turned as he asked and perused her face as if assessing the changes she made in her appearance. If he thought them nice or ill, he did not say.

"Yes, the south branch."

Sitting beside him, she told him everything about Isabela she and Hugh had learned and concluded. Whether he agreed with them, he did not say, but before he exhausted his questions, it was time for her to leave for work.

"Is your father home?"

"He's in his study. Down that path to the rear door of the church. After you enter, turn to the right. You will know at once if you have erred; you will find yourself in the sanctuary."

***

LAVINIA KEPT PHOEBE busy until just after noon when Asa and Hugh poked their heads into the writing room. "Honey, when's lunch?"

"Oh, I'm sorry. Phoebe and I have been catching up so furiously I hadn't noticed the time. Where are Clara and her beau?"

"Clara is on the veranda," answered Asa. "Wesley went to River Bend."

"Why, and why didn't she go with him?"

"Don't ask me." Asa glanced at Hugh.

"Me either. I guess he wanted to visit the colonel. Do we need to wait for him? We've been mending fences all morning, and I'm starved."

"I don't see why." Lavinia peeked at Hugh over the top of her glasses. "He knows when lunch is served. I'll pop into the kitchen and see if Mitilde is ready for us."

"What of Mr. Dyer?"

"Same goes for him. I can't play nursemaid to every stray who curls up in our barn." When she saw Phoebe's eyes grow larger, she smiled. "Don't mind me, Sugar. Just a figure of speech. We've given him his own room, though I do declare I shall be relieved if we ever again have our house to ourselves."

As her employer twirled away, Phoebe stuffed the envelope she just addressed, but Hugh lingered.

"You comin'?"

"In a moment—after I finish gathering the letters for the post office."

Once she joined the others, Mitilde brought them a platter of fried chicken. The men spoke of the distillery, and Lavinia of the correspondence they had yet to complete, leaving Clara little to do but fidget. When she was not playing with her food, she picked at a loose string in her napkin so persistently she elicited a sharp look from her mother.

"Clara, are you determined to unravel that hem? I grant you, those napkins aren't my favorites, but they are still serviceable. And you've barely touched your chicken."

"I'm sorry, Mother. I'm not very hungry."

Lavinia's expression softened. "Are you missing Wesley already—or perhaps coming down with a case of the jitters?"

"No, Mother. I just have…a few things on my mind." The glance she cast Phoebe looked like a plea.

"Your mother asked me to run some letters to town. Would you enjoy accompanying me—if it's all right with her, that is?"

"Yes, I think I would. It's a beautiful day, and I'd like to drop into Yancy's."

A slow smile spread across Lavinia's face. "That's a grand idea, though I'd be most appreciative if you two could deliver my letters to the post office before the afternoon train."

"Father, may we take the carriage?" Clara noticed Phoebe's surprise. "Riding in that old wagon of yours might wrinkle my skirt."

"Of course," answered Asa. "I'll ask Jubal to drive you in."

"I'll be happy to do it," suggested her brother, but his mother laid her hand on his.

"I believe your father wants your help, don't you, dear?"

"Uh…oh yes. I'd like you to help me draw up our partnership agreement with Wesley and determine what assets to include in Clara's dowry."

# Chapter 31

AS PHOEBE SITUATED herself across from Clara in the carriage, Jubal spoke through the open window. "Missy Phoebe, I put that pack of letters you is mailing in the box on the back, and Missus Lavinia asked me to include a parcel. She says you is to be particular that it gets delivered to the correct address."

When she leaned forward to inquire about its destination, Jubal peeked at Clara, who was gazing out the window opposite, and winked. What he intended, she could not confirm, but she nodded and sat back in her seat.

After they had pulled onto The Pike, Clara turned to her with an expression that announced she might burst if she delayed speaking any longer. "I have to ask you: what will become of Charles?"

"That will depend on any further evidence Mr. Dyer uncovers."

"But I leave in less than a week." Clara's eyes, normally a clear dark blue, clouded with despair. "I can't stand the thought of not knowing."

"Is it impossible for you to delay?"

Clara twisted her engagement ring around her finger. "You heard what my father said."

Phoebe had, but she easily could think of a more compelling reason. "Are your parents…forcing you?"

"Oh no, it's not what you are thinking."

"Do you love him?"

"What woman wouldn't? He is kind and gentle and treats me as if he thinks me the most treasurable woman alive. You know I would give anything to marry Charles, but that's out of the question—especially if he hangs from a rope."

As Clara thrust her face into her hands and wept, Phoebe switched to the carriage's other seat to slip an arm around her back. "Mr. Dyer is a fair man. He will not recommend charging Charles without sufficient evidence."

Clara began wagging her head. "That hateful woman was clutching one of his buttons."

"From whom did you hear that? It should have been kept confidential."

"Wesley." Sitting erect, she squirmed away from Phoebe. "If it's such a secret, how did you know?"

"I am sorry to say I identified it. If I hadn't, I'd have lost Mr. Jamison's trust, and then I could help Charles even less."

"Hmph. If Mr. Dyer is so fair, why is he detaining Charles when he has set that other man free? Button or not, it's as plain as the nose on your face that Whitcomb did it."

"How can you be so certain? He has acted a bit odd, but…"

"You heard her last words; besides, Wesley told my parents he is not to be trusted. All this time, Whitcomb's been acting as if the two of them are friends, but they only met over cards in my brother's club in New York."

"But Mr. Pinder seemed to be…"

"He has been cordial in deference to my family, Hugh first, and now all of us."

Sitting back against the carriage seat, Phoebe picked through the numerous occasions when she had seen the two together and discovered an error in her thinking. Not once had she witnessed a sign of intimacy between them. She, like Aunt Allison, had attributed Whitcomb's behavior to his title, which she now knew did not exist, and presumed Pinder tolerated him for the very same reason.

"Phoebe, will you promise to do something for me after we sail?"

"Of course. Anything."

"Visit Charles. He's in Old Bett's cabin. Please don't tell my parents, but I've been sneaking down there whenever I can get away. Although Wesley is *very* attentive, he's recently begun taking a long ride every day."

"He doesn't ask you to go with him?"

"Thankfully, no. Well, at least not constantly. Today I used our wedding preparations as an excuse."

The carriage pulled to a halt outside of the post office. "Missy Clara, we's here."

Once Jubal had leaped from the driver's box and opened the door, Clara headed toward the street. "You can find me at Yancy's when you are finished. I have a message for William."

Jubal handed Phoebe the small bundle of letters topped by the secret parcel. It was lightweight and thin enough to be posted, but across the top Lavinia had simply written: Mary Nelson. Phoebe slipped it into her knit bag, curiosity eating at her insides.

The letters took little time to mail. Only one man stood ahead of her, so while Jubal sat atop his box, she went to join Clara in Yancy's.

"…am just distraught with worry." Clara stopped speaking when she heard the shop-bell ring.

William Simmons glanced up at the same time. "Miss Farrell. Clara and I were discussing my brother."

"You need not explain to me."

"I suppose not, but I am frankly relieved you've come in. Hiram Hough, the postmaster, said a letter arrived for the dead woman yesterday afternoon." Both girl's eyes grew wide.

"He mentioned returning it to the sender, but since you are here, I wondered if you could speak with him."

"Oh, please do, Phoebe." Clara pressed her hands together, as if in prayer, but she was so excited, she began to bounce her fingertips off each other. "It might contain a clue that would free Charles."

"I am willing, but why would he give it to me?"

"I don't know. Perhaps because you are his pastor's daughter, and after all, she sought out *your* door. Besides, William said it was addressed to her at River Bend."

"That's odd. Who, beyond our circle, would know she was staying there? Perhaps, he will allow us to carry it to Mr. Dyer."

As the two young women scurried across the street, they saw Mr. Whitcomb entering the post office. He was arguing with Mr. Hough at the counter when Clara and Phoebe quietly slipped in.

"I tell you, my man, you must hand it over."

"I'm sorry, Sir Whitcomb. Only the recipient or the sender is entitled to read it unless you bring me an order from a judge."

"It's Mr. Whitcomb, not 'Sir', and I *am* the sender!"

Mr. Hough turned the letter so Mr. Whitcomb could read both addresses. "That's quite impossible. See? Richard Wilcox, County Sussex, England."

"I *am* Richard Wilcox."

"Then why have you been calling yourself Whitcomb and how could you have mailed this from England?" With that, he stashed the missive out of reach.

Whitcomb balled his hand into a fist so that Phoebe feared he might throw a blow across the counter at the postman's face.

Mr. Hough backed up a few steps. "Sir Whitcomb or Mr. Wilcox or whomever you are, I must ask you to leave the premises, or I will call the watchman, and if he doesn't stop you, he'll ride for Sheriff Hunter and toss you back into a cell. Don't think I'm unaware of where you spent the last few days. I was at The Lilacs' Saturday night. Speaking of the place, here's Miss Kiker now. Miss Farrell, did you forget something?"

"No sir. We wished to speak with you."

Whitcomb scowled from Clara to Phoebe and back at Mr. Hough again before he thrust open the door to the street.

"Now, young ladies, what may I do for you?"

Clara peered at Phoebe.

"I am afraid we already have our answer after hearing what you said to Mr. Whitcomb. William mentioned that letter while we were at Yancy's. They are still holding his brother Charles. Since the letter is addressed to River Bend, the three of us hoped you might entrust it to me since I am going there this evening or perhaps authorize me to carry it to Mr. Dyer. He is the private investigator assisting Judge Pennybacker."

Mr. Hough smiled. "I've known Charles since he was knee-high to a grasshopper and would bet my wagon he'd never do what they're accusing him of doing, but I'm afraid I can't give it to you any more than to that high-handed Englishman."

"Might you hold it until Mr. Dyer can gain a warrant from the judge?"

"Glad to, Missy. In fact, I'll stick it in the safe until that investigator brings me the authorization."

Clara reached over and squeezed the postmaster's arm. "Thank you, Mr. Hough. You are very kind."

"Just trying to carry out my duties in keeping with the law."

# Chapter 32

WHITCOMB WAS SITTING on the veranda when Jubal handed Clara and Phoebe down from the carriage. Once the two had come within a few feet of him, he rose. "Miss Farrell, will you walk through the garden with me?"

Phoebe glanced at Clara, hoping she might rescue her, but Pinder came through the door.

"Where have you been, pet?" He beamed affectionately as he kissed her hand. "I feared something might have happened."

As he guided Clara away, Whitcomb grasped Phoebe's wrist and threaded her arm through his. "Come, come, Miss Farrell. I thought you were an independent thinker. You are not going to get missish on me, are you? I promise not to compromise your morals."

"Why can we not talk here?"

"Too many people coming in and out." Holding her arm captive, he glided her down the steps while she looked back at the house and toward the barn. No one was about but Sari, who was beating a bedroom rug half-way around the back.

"Why did you follow me into the post office? You had delivered Lavinia's letters and gone onto the dry goods shop."

"I had a question for our postmaster." Phoebe tried to pull away, but he grasped her wrist tighter.

"I've no intention of hurting you." Whitcomb stopped and stared at her. "Provided you won't repeat what you heard."

"What about Clara?"

Whitcomb lifted his upper lip. "That little fool? She and her mother are so besotted with Pinder's title they fail to notice the obvious."

If that was what he had concluded, thought Phoebe, he was thickheaded and unobservant.

"You, on the other hand…"

"What about me?"

"Don't be vain, Miss Farrell; it doesn't suit you. Besides, I already expressed my opinion of you—the night of the ball, in this very spot."

Trying again to pull away, she found herself unexpectedly free. A dark hand had clamped her captor's shoulder and spun him around. Gripping him by the collar, Kitch lifted him to his toes. "You hurt, Missy Phoebe?"

She dimpled at her tall rescuer as Mr. Whitcomb sputtered.

"Why you…"

A whip's crack sent prickles up Phoebe's neck. "Let him go." The drawl was Asa Kiker's.

While all three whirled around, Whitcomb pointed at Kitch. "Your slave attacked me."

As quick as she might, Phoebe pushed between them. "No, sir. He came to my rescue."

For a few tense moments, Mr. Kiker flicked his eyes from one to the other, settling his piercing glare on

Whitcomb. "Pack your bags. You've overstayed your welcome."

"I can't. That inspector has my traveling papers."

"You won't need them to rent a room. There's a tavern in town."

"Lord Dunham," Whitcomb snarled, "will not take kindly to this!"

As he strode toward the house, Phoebe caught the look Asa Kiker flashed Kitch. It held respect she had not expected, but as he turned toward her, his forehead crumpled.

"Are you alright?"

"I'm fine, sir, though I appreciate Kitch coming when he did."

While Mr. Kiker guided her to the steps, he nodded toward the writing room window. Mr. Dyer was framed within it, watching. "It appears you have a second guardian." Tipping his hat, he returned to his mount.

Ignoring Dyer, Phoebe ran after her champion as he was walking around back toward the kitchen garden. "Thank you for…for *all* you risked. How did you know I needed help?"

Kitch tossed his eyes toward the house. "Them walls got eyes and ears, Missy Phoebe. Long as you stays close, you's safe."

"But we were on the other side of the lilac trees."

Kitch's grin lit his face. "Sari be watchin' you as she beat that rug an' sees you ain't keen on that man's company. She run to fetch me."

As something caught his eye, he bobbed his head toward the veranda. "Missus Lavinia be over yonder, lookin' for you. She's wavin' up a storm."

Phoebe turned to see Mrs. Kiker leaning over the rail.

"Come inside. Mr. Dyer here has been asking after you. After our hard work this morning, I have nothing left for you to do, so I said he is welcome to use my writing room. Would you like to stay for dinner?"

"Um…" Phoebe fingered the reticule dangling from her arm. "I promised to drop something by River Bend this evening."

Mr. Dyer stepped onto the porch. "May I accompany you?"

Phoebe felt caught. If she said no, she might rouse his suspicion, but she dare not say yes. She was not sure what the parcel she carried contained, but Lavinia quite obviously wished to keep it secret.

Mrs. Kiker cut in. "Why Mr. Dyer, how very gallant, especially after what just happened to our dear Phoebe, but she won't be travelling alone. The Nelsons invited Mr. Auger to dinner."

Phoebe whipped her head toward Lavinia.

"Honey, how many times must I tell you to close that pretty little mouth. You are bound to catch flies. And to answer the question I can see you are formulating, Whitcomb stomped in here with smoke flaring from his nostrils."

"Oh, that reminds me. I need to find Sari."

"She went upstairs."

As Phoebe grasped the knoll-post, Lavinia turned to Mr. Dyer with her most generous smile. "What were you saying, sir?"

# Chapter 33

PHOEBE FOUND SARI in a room she guessed was Hugh's, restoring the rug to its proper place. The walls were a deep blue green that reminded her of spruce trees, the furniture and paneling were of polished maple, and a peg she could see in the dressing room held an oil skin cape. Not wishing to intrude, she stood framed by the doorway.

"Thank you." She smiled when the girl glanced up. "That Mr. Whitcomb is odious."

Sari flicked her a look that announced her agreement before breaking into a wide grin. "You got friends, Missy. More 'an you know."

Phoebe flushed with pleasure at the unexpected revelation. Though sure of Mitilde and Kitch's attachment, their extended family treated her with the respectful reserve they showed all guests within The Lilacs. "And you have one in me, Sari."

The girl ducked her head, as if she felt as vulnerable as Phoebe, and resumed finger-combing the fringe on the end of the carpet.

As Phoebe recalled her last trip upstairs, she leaned against the doorframe. "Was Mr. Whitcomb staying in the room across the hall?"

Sari raised up. "The one beside Mr. and Mrs. Kiker? That room belongs to Missy Clara's beau. You needs sumthin' from it?"

"No, but I hoped you might clear up a question for me. A day or two after the Englishmen arrived, Mrs. Kiker asked me to fetch her glasses from her side table. While I did, I heard drawers opening in the room you've just told me is Mr. Pinder's. I'd assumed you might be putting away laundry, since most of the guests had gone into town, but not three minutes later, I collided with Mr. Whitcomb in the hall."

When the girl glanced hesitantly toward Hugh's open door, Phoebe stepped inside and shut it.

"No miss. First laundry I done for Mr. Pinder was last week." Her eyes darted again toward the doorway.

"What is it, Sari? Have you seen something?"

"Not seen, heard. Wasn't meanin' to listen, you understand, but I's in Mr. Auger's room polishin' a mirror when I hears that Mr. Whitcomb talking real low and mean, sort of like a bobcat growlin'."

"Did you hear what he said?"

"Yes'm, I hear 'xactly: 'If you don't, I will.'"

"Will what?"

"Don't know, but Missy Clara's beau ask real soft-like: 'Is you threatenin' me?' an' then warned him never to do it again. Next thing I hears is a door shuttin' an' footsteps down the hall."

"Thank you for telling me, Sari."

"You is sure welcome. Ain't none of us fond of a man tasked with overseein,' Missy Phoebe, but don't mean we want to see Mr. Charles strung up. He's a sight better than that daddy of his was, and ain't nobody been whipped since…since someone done that man in."

"If you hear or see anything else that strikes you as odd—anything at all—please find me right away."

Sari sat back on her heels. "Maybe I did see somethin'. Gentlemen gots a habit of burnin' things, but mostly they burns letters an' such."

"What did one of them burn?"

"A real fine shirt, the kind they wears to the Kikers' fancy parties."

"When?"

The girl scratched her head. "Sunday last, in the mornin'. Night after that woman be strangled. I goes into that English guest's room to see if he's left food out on his table. He do that sometimes. Missus Lavinia says we is free to take our day of rest, but food draws mice an' nobody want that. I smells ash an' thinks, 'who be lightin' a fire in this heat?' When I checks the grate, sure enough, I find the collar of one of them shirts I told you about, mostly burned clean through, laying in a heap of ash."

"What did you do with it?"

"Sweep it up and toss it in the ash bin like always."

Phoebe's mind began to whir.

"You said the guest was English. Which one?"

"Same as pulled you out into the garden."

"What happens to the ashes once you sweep them into the bin?"

"They all gets sifted together and shaked onto the rye. One of my little brother's jobs."

"And the collar? What would've happened to it?"

Sari hung her head. "I tooks it, Missy Phoebe. Thought my mamma might be able to least salvage a part to line the collar of a coat."

"Do you think you could bring it back?"

"I ain't stold it. Missus Lavinia say we can keep somethin' if we find it with the trash."

"I didn't think you had, but if Mr. Dyer could look at it, he might notice something that would free Mr. Simmons. Fine shirts are expensive. Mr. Whitcomb may be wealthy, but not so rich he can burn them instead of putting them with the wash."

"I'll go see soon as I can get away. I gots potatoes to peel after I's through up here."

"I appreciate all you have told me. If you find it, please take it directly to Mr. Dyer. I will tell him to expect you and why."

When Phoebe slipped back into the hallway, she came face to face with Mr. Auger. He took a step back, his neck coloring as he noted whose room she was exiting.

"Oh. Hello, Aaron." She swung the door wide so he could not miss its occupant. "I was talking with Sari."

"Lavinia said I might find you up here. If you will give me a moment to refresh my attire, I will escort you to the Nelsons'. The whole house is talking about Mr. Whitcomb's sudden departure. Perhaps you might fill me in on the event that precipitated it on the way there."

"After I ask Kitch to ready my wagon, I'll meet you on the veranda."

Swishing down the staircase, she smacked straight into Mr. Dyer, who, though he steadied her, did not let her go.

"Miss Farrell, I seem to remember us doing this on the Auger's staircase."

Phoebe might have dimpled had her discoveries not been urgent. "I appear to be prone to collisions. Perhaps I need to look up more as I am walking. Do you have a moment?"

"I can make one. Have you learned something?"

After she had finished relating all Sari had confided, Mr. Dyer remained immobile, gazing down at her, though she suspected he was entangled in his own thoughts. After a few moments, he found his way out of them. "That is most interesting. Whitcomb cannot have burned it. Judge Pennybacker detained him immediately after the victim was discovered."

"Who then?"

"Unless Jamison locked Whitcomb's room, it might have been anyone staying in this home." His eyes lit as he peered into hers. "Or anyone who had access to it."

Phoebe glanced away lest he see how his teasing affected her, but when she returned her attention to him, he had grown serious.

"That means I must reassess your friend Mr. Auger. I had the distinct impression earlier that Mrs. Kiker was trying to prevent me from accompanying the two of you to…what is the name of the place you are going?"

"River Bend. Colonel and Mary Nelson's home."

"Was she attempting to protect you or Mr. Auger?"

"Why should she be protecting either of us? I have nothing to fear from you, and Mr. Auger has nothing to fear from the Nelsons. I am certain he will enjoy dining with both them and their granddaughter, Emily. She is a lovely young woman."

The twitch of Mr. Dyer's brow might have been involuntary and smoothed out so quickly it might not have happened. "If he is going there already, can't you hand off your errand and save yourself the journey?"

"River Bend is not far past the parsonage, and Mr. Auger is not the only one who wishes to see Emily."

"So *you* will not protest if I also escort you? I have questions for your father."

"Oh." She feared he noticed her disappointment. "He should be home. He starts to prepare his sermons on Wednesdays."

Inclining his head in a brief bow, Mr. Dyer excused himself to see about a mount.

# Chapter 34

WHEN PHOEBE AND her two escorts arrived at River Bend, Papa Nelson invited Dyer to his study. She suspected Aaron played a hand in this. Whether for his own purposes or Lavinia's, he had dismounted ahead of Mr. Dyer and spoken to the colonel directly before taking Emily's arm and leading her downstream.

Phoebe handed Mary Nelson Lavinia's parcel. "This is for you."

"What's in it?"

"Mrs. Kiker didn't say, but she took pains to ensure only Jubal was aware she had sent it. Neither she nor I could deter Mr. Dyer from accompanying me."

"I noticed the two of you, thick as thieves, talking in the corner during Clara's engagement party."

"He helped Matthew Bentley when Mrs. Auger passed away."

"As did you from what I hear. So, what do you think of him?"

Phoebe felt the color creeping up her neck. "He is intelligent and perceptive."

Mrs. Nelson's eyes began to twinkle. "I wasn't asking about his skills."

"Oh." Phoebe glanced away. "Mr. Bentley speaks well of him."

"Alright. I can take a hint, but I can also see a spark between the two of you that has nothing to do with *detecting.*"

Happily, for Phoebe, Sally chose that minute to clarify an item on the Nelson's dinner menu, and Papa Nelson opened his study door.

"Are you sure that's all you want?" asked Gary, escorting Mr. Dyer to the parlor. "Mr. Jamison asked me the same questions."

Spotting Phoebe, Mr. Dyer's smile turned a little sheepish. "I wanted to hear it from you directly."

"Now you know where to find me. You are welcome at any time. Are you sure we cannot persuade you to join us for dinner? Phoebe, you are wanted also."

"Thank you, Papa Nelson, but I can't. My parents are expecting me, and I wouldn't want to cause them any worry. Besides, I would imagine you are looking forward to a quieter evening."

"We have had an unusual amount of people dropping in."

"Mr. Kiker told us Lord Dunham visited you this morning."

"Yes." The colonel's blue eyes, which had been warm with affection, cooled. "I thought it rather odd. I was just telling Mr. Dyer. He asked me to stand up with him at the wedding."

"Why, Gary," Mama Nelson said, "you didn't tell me."

"I haven't had a chance. "

"He barely knows you. I would have thought he'd have asked Hugh or Aaron." She spun her head toward Mr. Auger as he and Emily came in.

"He claimed it was a gesture of friendship between countries—to honor my military service. If you are sure the two of you won't stay for dinner, we will see you on Saturday."

"Phoebe," asked Emily, "what are you wearing to the wedding?"

"I haven't given it any thought. What is customary?"

"I am wearing my finest day frock, the one I wore for the Kikers' last tea."

"Then I will wear mine also—and thank you."

As Phoebe and Mr. Dyer descended the single porch step, he angled his head to study her expression. "I felt like I missed something in that last exchange."

"Emily was alerting me to the expected dress for Saturday. She knows I wouldn't have given it thought until that morning."

"Then we are alike, Miss Farrell. Though now that you bring it to my attention, I am not sure I am invited. I was only at the engagement party because of this woman's murder." He helped her into the wagon.

"Do you wish to be?"

Mr. Dyer paused. "Perhaps, perhaps not. It would give me a chance to search the suspects' rooms unhindered. If the Kikers will not mind, I may make a showing at the reception afterward."

"You mistrust the Kikers? They might mind very much to know you are fumbling through their possessions."

"They are not on my list."

"Who then?"

"After what Sari said, your friend, Aaron Auger, for one."

"You surely cannot doubt him. He is also a long-time friend of Matthew Bentley's, and you are riding *his* horse."

"Your point?"

Phoebe's mouth dropped open, though she hastily shut it. If Lavinia were present, she would ask if Phoebe intended to catch flies. "Matthew would never…"

He lifted one brow as he waited for her to finish.

"I suppose their friendship doesn't disqualify him."

"Most murderers know their victims well."

"That surely mitigates against him and also Charles."

"Does it?"

"You have discovered something."

By then, he was mounting his borrowed horse, and after a few short minutes was riding up The Pike beside her.

"Mr. Dyer, I told you everything I have learned, but you have not returned the favor."

"No, I have not, Miss Farrell. Nor do I intend to."

***

AS AUGIE PASSED his father a bowl of late greens, the reverend watched his daughter.

"You appear wearier than usual, Kitten. Hard day?"

"More like a hard week. What did Mr. Dyer want of you?"

"A few clarifications, nothing more."

"Oh," sighed Amelia. "Can we please talk of something besides this murder?"

"Yes, Mama, and I do have lovely news. The friend I mentioned, the one who intentionally embarrassed me, asked for my forgiveness."

Her mother set down her glass. "Well, I'm delighted, and I can see you are also. Your dimples always twitch when you are happy."

"I am, at least about that."

"So, it *was* Virginia," declared Augie. "It had to have been. The two of you walked off by yourself yesterday and didn't come back for a good half hour."

"August," responded his father. "You know better than to ask. We were all through this less than two weeks ago."

"But she said it's all resolved."

"Since you haven't a good reason to know, it would still be gossip."

"So? Why the big fuss over a little gossip?"

"Your father is right, son. A little gossip is like a small lie: a tiny seed that reaps a great harvest once planted. You may think it will not hurt, but it might forever erode your regard for the young woman."

"Not knowin' erodes it more! If I don't know which of the Simmons sisters is guilty, I'll distrust all three."

"You are proving Papa's point, not negating it. If I'd never confided someone hurt me, you wouldn't suspect anyone at all. That's why I never confirmed your misgivings in the first place. Yes, I saw the Simmonses that day, but in any given day at The Lilacs, I see any number of friends and acquaintances."

Reverend Farrell set down his lemonade. "Relationships are precious things, whether with a friend, a family member, or even a very kind gardener. Better to guard them well from any danger that might break them." He paused to take another sip. "That reminds me, Amelia. The last time we discussed forgiveness, Foster paid us a visit. Do you know if he has found his spade?"

While Amelia shook her head, Phoebe heard her brother gulp.

"Ernest, when I misplaced my thimble, I asked the Lord where it was; and not ten minutes later, I found it in my blue apron pocket."

Phoebe glanced at her father. "Do you think He cares to hear about little things like that?"

"I can speak only as a parent: if a matter is important to one of my children, it's important to me—and I suspect this particular spade has garnered His special notice." He tossed his eyes toward Augie and laid his hands, palms up, on the table. "Shall we ask the Lord where it is? Well-crafted tools are hard to come by."

Augie stared at his father's hand for a moment, unable to bring himself to hold it. "Papa, I need to say something before we pray."

"Go ahead, son. We are all ears."

"I—I need to ask Foster to forgive me." His head drooped lower. "I lied to him…about the spade. I know where it is."

"Go on."

"I was usin' it to dig for worms and left it out in the rain. It was all rusty when I went back for it, and I was afraid Foster would be mad."

"Where is it?"

"I buried it down by the river."

"Well, I believe I saw him putting compost around the peony bushes along the front of the church. Let's go see if he has time to talk."

"Now?"

"Better get it done. If not, it may fester like a boil beneath your britches, but it's up to you."

"Alright. I want to be able to look Foster in the eye."

# Chapter 35

AUGIE KNOCKED BACK the kitchen door with a thud, startling his sister as she set the table for breakfast.

"Watch it! I nearly dropped the bowls."

"Look what I found!" He held out his hands, displaying a grimy twisted ribbon and a familiar cameo brooch.

"Where did you get *that*? It's Mama Nelson's!"

"Isabela was wearing it at the ball."

"Are you sure?"

"As sure as can be. I danced with her."

"Here, Augie, let's wrap them in this towel so I can take them to Mr. Dyer."

"Nuh-uh! *I'm* taking them to him myself. He'll probably want to ask me all sorts of questions."

"You are right. Where did you find them?"

"I don't want to say until I talk with Mr. Dyer. Matthew Bentley said, 'The first time a testimony is given is usually the most accurate.'"

"Good point. You can ride up with me after breakfast and maybe he'll bring you home. Mr. Auger has given him the use of a mount."

"Yeah. I bet he'll want to see for himself where I dug it up, but let's go now. Mama will understand."

In all her life—or his, rather—Phoebe could not recall her brother being so excited that he was happy to skip a meal. After they consulted with their parents, they set off for The Lilacs.

***

MR. DYER USHERED the brother and sister into Lavinia's writing room. Taking the seat behind the desk, he indicated Augie should sit directly in front of him and then stood up again. The room was too tiny to house many pieces of furniture. "Miss Farrell, would you care to sit in Mrs. Kiker's chair, that is if your brother doesn't mind you staying."

Augie's eyes glimmered. "I guess she can as long as she doesn't make herself… Phoebe, what did you say Mr. Jamison called you?"

Without replying, his sister slipped into Lavinia's damask covered chair, though she would like to have pinched his neck.

Mr. Dyer's lips tilted. "The word was 'nuisance.'" Closing the door, he removed a graphite pencil and small pad from his coat pocket, crossed to the recessed window, leaned against the ledge, and flipped to a clean page. "For the record, what is your full name?"

"August Timothy Farrell."

"Timothy? I have a brother by that name." He looked at Phoebe as if he thought the information might interest her, then recalling himself he tilted his pencil toward the items atop the towel on the desk. "Please state exactly what these are, if you're able to identify them, and how they came to be in your possession."

"Yes, sir. The brooch is called a cameo because of the lady's face carved into it. See?"

"I am familiar with them. Continue."

"Isabela—the woman who was staying with the Nelsons—wore it to the Kikers' ball this past Saturday. My sister told me it belongs to Mrs. Nelson."

When the inspector lifted his chin toward Phoebe, she nodded. "It can be no other. Papa Nelson—the colonel—gave it to her on their last anniversary. The reverse side will be inscribed: 'To Mary with devotion, Gary.'"

Both retrieving and turning it over, he cocked a brow. "I am surprised Mrs. Nelson would lend such a valuable gift. Extraordinarily generous."

Augie bounced to the edge of his chair. "Not for Mama Nelson. Tell him Phoebe. She's like a bevelonant queen in a fairy tale."

"Benevolent," his sister corrected.

"And Papa Nelson, too. He gave me one of his favorite fishing rods last week."

Dyer looked at Phoebe.

"You would not be surprised if you knew her well. Of course, when she lent it, she did not expect the borrower to…be unable to return it the same evening."

"And the ribbon?"

"I could not say." She bent over the object but was hesitant to pick it up. "Augie, do you remember the color of Isabela's dress?"

He narrowed his eyes. "Green, sort of like a baking apple."

Mr. Dyer flipped over the ribbon with his graphite. The entire length was wrinkled and looked as if it had been soaked in mud, yet a clear quarter inch of its original color showed beneath each end where either the victim or one of her hostesses had turned and finished its cut edges.

"Please do not mention either of these to anyone. I'll ride down to River Bend so Mrs. Nelson can verify they are hers and that the murdered woman wore both that night. Mr. Farrell, do you think you could show me where you found them?"

"Sure. I dug them up from our riverbank when I…"

Silently, Mr. Dyer waited for him to finish.

"I had hidden something in the same place."

"What was it?"

Augie tossed his eyes toward his sister. "I have a small chest that I bury my…treasures in."

"And you think whoever hid these items has seen you?"

"How should I know? No—they couldn't have. I hid Foster's spade close to a month ago, but maybe they spotted the overturned grass or something."

Mr. Dyer arched a brow. "You buried someone's spade in your treasure chest?"

"Not in it, but in the same place."

"Perhaps," offered Phoebe, the man was in a hurry. Sticking these items in Augie's hole might have been easier than digging a fresh one."

"Undoubtedly, and it may have offered an additional benefit: by hiding the murder weapon with your stash, they may have hoped to implicate you."

"Me? I'm nine years old. Who would believe I would or even could…"

"The killer may have assumed the chest belonged to this gardener of yours or even your father."

"What a rotten thing to do!"

"A man—or woman—who commits murder wouldn't have scruples against indicating another for his crime."

"A woman?" Phoebe blinked.

"Doubtful, but not impossible. If we assume Charles Simmons is telling the truth, a woman might have come up behind and hit him with a shovel. There are several long-handled tools in the place. Then if she grabbed the victim from behind…" He trailed off when he noticed the expressions on the Farrell children's faces. "Can you think of a woman who might have a motive?"

"No one," replied Phoebe, though she instantly realized that was not true. "I suppose maybe Clara. She has long wanted to marry Charles, and he was paying an extraordinary amount of attention to Isabela."

"Clara?" Augie made a face. "She would never take a shovel to him. She might have killed him."

"What do you think, Miss Farrell? Considering her impending nuptials, I had assumed her attached to Lord Dunham."

Phoebe did not at first answer. Although she might not feel close to Clara, Lavinia would be heartbroken. However, last year she had crossed a murderer off a list of suspects for a similar reason and promised herself never to do so again. "If, as you say, we accept Charles's version of Saturday night—and he did have a large lump on his head—I must agree with Augie. She would not have risked killing him."

"Miss Kiker would not be the first spurned female to wish her…object of affection…dead, especially if she caught them…" He let the suggestion fall as he flicked his eyes from Phoebe to her brother. One was a child and the other, for all her composure, was not many years beyond that state.

"Wait a minute!" Augie sat up. "If Clara knocked him out, how was she able to shove him on top of Blaze? It took all four of us to lift him into our wagon."

Mr. Dyer rubbed his lip. "Good question, and that theory does rely heavily on Charles's account of events. He might have received that lump any number of ways, and he is well-acquainted with the church park. Isn't it near the place your family found him? He may have hidden this evidence and been on his way home when his horse was spooked."

When neither of the Farrell children answered, he looked at the clock ticking away the seconds. "It's already ten. Augie, why don't you show me that spot where you bury your treasures and let your sister start her workday."

Once the boy bounded through the door, Mr. Dyer returned his attention to Phoebe. "Do you think it at all odd Miss Kiker agreed so readily to leave her family for a man she—according to you—does not love? Sailing to England would put her well out of Judge Pennybacker's reach."

"A woman may have many reasons to marry. He *is* an earl."

Mr. Dyer smiled down at her. "And you, Miss Farrell? What do you look for in a husband?"

Phoebe dropped her eyes, unsure if he wanted a serious answer or meant to tease; but before she could decide, a wrap at the door jolted them apart. As he stuck his head around the jamb, he found a familiar dark-skinned girl of about Phoebe's age.

"I's lookin' for Missy Phoebe."

"I'm here, Sari. Have you met Mr. Dyer?"

"I's seen him." She held out the charred shirt collar. "I's bringin' this for her to give to you. It gots some initials sewn into it. Right here."

"Thank you." Dyer took it from the girl's hands.

"You's welcome, sir. Can I go? Mitilde be wanting me in the kitchen."

"Go ahead. I will keep it safe."

While Sari scurried down the hall, Phoebe pressed closer to see the item clearly. "RWW. We cannot doubt whose initials they are. We know no one else who shares them. Surely, they clear Clara."

"Do they? I am aware of your regard for the Kikers, but doesn't this strike you as a little convenient? Why thoroughly burn the shirt but leave the one identifying part intact?"

Phoebe considered what he was saying. Clara had means, motive, and might have easily slipped into the barn between dances. "You think she is purposefully trying to implicate Whitcomb?"

"If not her, someone is. Each of the Kikers can move freely about the house without raising a single eyebrow."

"But none of them could have made Isabela murmur the man's name."

"No, but if someone wanted to cast suspicion away from themselves, wouldn't that make him the most obvious person to blame?"

When Phoebe said nothing in reply, he again craned his neck around the door frame. "I'd best find your brother; but think about it. I value your opinion. Until then, I bid you good day."

# Chapter 36

ASA KIKER OPENED the writing room door. "Lavinia, where on earth has Jubal gotten to? I need him to drive me into town."

Lavinia tilted her head. "Have you tried his quarters or asked after him in the kitchen?"

"Of course, I have. No one has seen him since last evening. He did not show up at the distillery."

"What about Wesley and Clara? Mitilde made dinner for Lisa and Jordan White, and Clara wanted to bring little Luke a present. They may have asked him to drive them."

Asa thrust his hands into his pockets. "How many times must I tell her to check with me first? I have an important meeting for which I prefer to be fresh."

"Oh, Darling, they are young and in love. Besides, I've always thought you look so rugged and handsome when your clothes are less starched and a breeze has ruffled your hair. The stiffly formal gentleman doesn't suit you."

Phoebe, who could not avoid hearing the conversation in a room so small, pretended to be absorbed by the letters she was sealing. She had the impression Mr. Kiker was embarrassed, though whether by his display of irritation or his wife's lavish admiration was harder to discern. She suspected the latter and had an equally distinct impression Lavinia, though expressing how she honestly felt, had used it to redirect his attention. The reason, she hoped, would fill Ruby with joy.

"I doubt the men I'm meeting will assess me by your criteria. Any idea how long they will be? I can't wait more than half past."

"Oh, I just remembered. Wesley mentioned picking up something—a piece of jewelry, I'd guess—that he commissioned as a wedding present for Clara, so we will not see them as soon as that."

"Alright. I won't be back until late, so don't hold dinner."

When he turned to leave, Lavinia circled around the desk. "Asa, I forgot to tell you: that investigator has cleared Aaron to leave. He has been anxious to go for several days, so I assume he will not be here when you return."

"Well, if not, please give him my best wishes, and Phoebe, I doubt I'll see you tomorrow. Lavinia tells me the bunch of you ladies will be decorating the church, so I'll see you at the wedding."

"I hope your meeting goes well, Mr. Kiker." As she watched him exit into the hall, Phoebe inwardly smiled. Unless she was truly dense and altogether missing something, Aaron's departure confirmed her happy expectations of a few minutes ago. She was not the least surprised that the news also carried with it a sense of loss. Aaron had become such an everyday part of her recent life. What concerned her more was Emily. The two had had less than a week to cement their regard for one another. Perhaps that would change with time.

While she was tucking the completed correspondence into the mail pouch, Mr. Dyer stuck his head through the door and held up a familiar looking envelope. "The judge issued the order this morning."

"Is that the letter Whitcomb was trying to bully our postmaster into giving him?"

"Yes, I've just come from there."

She was pleased he confided this to her and was tempted to ask to see it, but he slipped it back into his frock coat. "Have you pinned down which Englishmen was pressing William Simmons for information?"

"Lord Dunham denies ever having spoken with him outside of an introduction at Saturday's ball. He admits to exploring shops in the town but cannot say whether Yancy's was one of them."

"What of Whitcomb?"

"Vanished."

"What do you mean? He said you had kept his traveling papers."

Irritation showed clearly on Mr. Dyer's normally impassive face. "I'd hired that slave-catcher Spry to tail him, but it appears either he is poor at his work or Whitcomb is clever. When the tavern maid went to clean his room, he'd cleared out."

"My father says running is a sign of guilt."

"Often." He patted his coat pocket. "I will know more once I read this."

"Did you learn anything from exploring the church park?"

He shook his head. "Too many regular footsteps up the paths closer to your house, and we could find nothing but your brother's cache by the river."

"Excuse me," murmured Lavinia from over his shoulder. "I need to get into my writing room."

"Of course." Mr. Dyer stood aside. "Miss Farrell and I are finished, and I am due elsewhere." Bobbing his head politely, he turned and left.

As his footsteps snapped down the hall, Mrs. Kiker craned her neck to make sure he was out of hearing. "I am not sure what to make of that man. Matthew was so charming. This man makes me feel as if I am being watched."

"I would guess that you are, along with all of us. Sadly, the time I spent at the Auger's last yuletide taught me that the last person you might suspect, given sufficient reason, was capable of unspeakable deeds."

Lavinia paused as if what Phoebe said had set her on the trail of an interesting notion, but rather than reveal it, she dropped her eyes to the mail pouch. "Let us wrap up for the day, Sugar. Mr. Kiker will be home late, and I have some…wedding plans to attend to."

***

WHEN EMILY SAW Phoebe tie Esmeralda to River Bend's post, she sprang off the swing on which she had been reading and scurried over the small stone bridge.

"I'm delighted to see you, Phoebe. Why don't you pull into the stable yard?"

"I cannot stay long. Mrs. Kiker told me Mr. Auger is returning to Pennsylvania. Are you alright?"

"I am." She grabbed Phoebe's hands and pulled her closer. "He is here, now, in Grandfather's study."

"Oh, Emily!" Phoebe dimpled deeply. "He is an honorable man, and anyone can tell he thinks you appealing."

Emily's blush covered each inch of skin from her throat to her hairline. "I still cannot believe it."

"Were he not serious about his intentions, he would not take this step."

As Emily listened, the sparkle in her eyes dimmed a bit. "But am I second choice? He came here for you, not me. Had you not refused him…"

"Oh, Emily, are you so unaware of the treasure you are? He merely met me first and would soon have discovered how little I would suit him. Honestly, given a choice between the two of us, you could never come in second."

"Phoebe, you mustn't say such things. If it is true—and I'm not saying it is—that's only because God has designed you to suit some other man better. But I don't want to get ahead of myself. For all I know, he is speaking with Grandfather about Ju…" Her hand flew over her mouth as she realized her carelessness.

"Don't worry on either account. I've already figured out Mr. Auger's place in…our local endeavors and couldn't be happier for…Ruby. Perhaps, he seeks only to get to know you better as he did with me, but he is not insensible. When he asked to speak with your grandfather privately, he knew what suspicions he would arouse."

"Who could have imagined while we were becoming friends last year, that you would accept a position that might alter *my* life forever? And what of you? Grandmother suspects you find Mr. Dyer…interesting."

"I do, but I now know better than to assume an attraction is mutual. Besides, after this investigation is concluded, I doubt I will ever cross paths with him again."

Emily's lips twisted playfully. "You never know. If I happen one day to move to Allentown, I will invite him to dinner whenever you are visiting. Can you stay, at least long enough to bid Mr. Auger farewell?"

"Only for a few minutes."

Before they had each settled on a swing, the side door opened and out strode the colonel. "Emily's out here, Mary, and we have a visitor."

His expression brought a gleeful fairy tale elf to Phoebe's mind, but when she saw Aaron looking awkward, she yielded the place beside Emily. "I was leaving, though I am glad to see you, Aaron, before you go. I'll just pop inside and say hello to Mama Nelson."

When no one tried to convince her to stay, she knew what the outcome of the discussion in the study must have been and happily took her leave.

# Chapter 37

REVEREND FARRELL PASSED his daughter a platter of eggs scrambled with fried potatoes and onions.

"You and your mother have a big day ahead of you. Amelia, after breakfast, I'll fetch a goose from the smokehouse."

"Thank you, dear. You have read my mind. I want to finish all the lunch preparations I can before Lavinia and Allison arrive. Kitten, when did she tell you we may expect them?"

"Mid-morning. She, Mrs. Wilson, and Sari plan to cut every flower still blooming at The Lilacs, which will not be many. I'm going to bundle them with beech branches. Our maples and oaks have shed most of their leaves."

"You might add some dogwood berries, and I saw a sweet gum toward the bottom of Simmons Lane. Its bright scarlet leaves would be a gorgeous addition."

"After I get the goose, Augie and I can take the wagon over and ask Mahala if we can clip some for you. What do you say, son?"

"I'd like it fine, but will *they*—with Charles locked up and all, and that duke stealing Clara?"

"He is an earl, dear, and Virginia is standing up with Clara. I do so appreciate your thoughtfulness, though. You are growing into an admirable young man."

Although Augie trained his eyes on his eggs, Phoebe noticed he was smiling. She also noted how deftly her mother had sidestepped his question. Glancing at her father, she saw he had stopped eating and was worrying his mustache.

"Papa, is something bothering you?"

"What? Oh. No, Kitten. Well, sort of. When I ran into Asa in town yesterday, he told me Jubal is missing."

She flicked her brother a warning glance. "I don't think there is anything to worry about. When Mr. Kiker came searching for him, Mrs. Kiker suggested he had driven Clara and her fiancé to the Whites. Come to think of it, Hugh was absent from the Lilacs yesterday."

Augie flung his eyes toward the ceiling. "Mr. Kiker would know if Jubal was with Hugh."

"Mind your tone with your sister, dear. She was just offering an idea. Ernest, did Asa say how long he'd been missing?"

"I can't recall. Not for long."

Phoebe remembered precisely, but to say so might provoke more questions. "Do you know who else is missing? Richard Whitcomb."

"That dreadful Englishman I suggested you dance with?"

"Mama, you were just trying to be kind, but yes—him."

Papa's eyes looked like they might pop. "What do you mean, 'missing,' Kitten?"

"When Mr. Dyer went to the tavern yesterday, he discovered Whitcomb had slipped away either in the night or early hours of the morning. Mr. Spry never spotted him leaving."

"That slave catcher is working for Dyer? Well, I must say, I am glad to hear it. Lavinia was likely right about Clara employing Jubal, but on the off chance he has fled—and I'm only mentioning it as a possibility—he chose an opportune time."

***

PHOEBE OPENED HER window several inches, hoping to catch a breeze, then fell, exhausted, into bed. Lavinia and Allison had used every flower Sari and they found to create a bouquet for Clara; and Mama, Mary, Emily, and she had sufficient leaves and berries left over to assemble and attach nosegays to the ends of each pew that faced the center aisle. Even Augie had been helpful, scouring the trunks in the attic for cast off pieces of ribbon that might match or compliment the fall hues. The effect was reminiscent of a snug copse of autumn trees.

As she fluffed the pillow, she pondered a statement Lavinia made that day to Augie. It was something about him adding the items he found by the river to his box of treasures. Whatever would put such a notion in Lavinia's head, unless she had misheard something Mr. Dyer said? She was surprised he would say anything at all, but there was no use fretting over it now.

Turning onto her side, she began wondering how close Jubal and Aaron Auger were to Mason and Dixon's line. She had surmised the parcel she had delivered to Mary contained Jubal's identification papers, but until he crossed into a free state, they could not be assured of his safety. As she began to pray for both, her speech became slurred by sleep, and she was soon dragged into its depths.

***

RAIN PELTED PHOEBE'S window, followed by a crack of thunder so loud she sat upright. Jumping out of bed, she bounded over to close the gap she had left open and was rewarded with a sharp gust spitting rain onto her nightdress. Shivering, she shoved against the swollen sill. It barely budged before a bolt of lightning brightened the sky. She froze.

"Phoebe." Augie stood in her doorway. "Why are you just standing there? That window won't close itself."

She was shaking so hard her lips began to tremble. "I…I…"

While she stared, transfixed, out the window, he crossed the room and grasped the middle rail. "Come on, help me."

"Is...is that…"

"What?" Augie peered through the glass over the parsonage park, but storm clouds had shrouded the waning moon with darkness. "I can't see anything. Together, on the count of three. One, two, three."

When they shoved the sash into place, a second strike pierced the darkness. Phoebe grabbed Augie's night shirt, yanking his face closer to the window. "There!" Down by the river, a hunched form was digging in the soaked bank.

A third bolt lit the sky, showing a man struggling to yank a box from the sucking mud.

"That's my treasure chest!" As Augie darted from her side, Phoebe shot out a hand and dragged him back. "You can't. He's killed once; he'll have no qualms about hurting you."

"Let's at least run down to the parlor and see if we can catch a closer glimpse."

As they started to turn, the wind whisked a cloud aside, allowing them to see someone lumbering up the bank. Phoebe's heart thumped hard against her chest. "Hugh!"

While another cloud covered the park in darkness, Augie grasped his sister's hand, pulled her into the hall, down the stairs, and into the parlor.

Phoebe peered out the back window as her brother ran around front to see if he could spot the man's mount, but while he was shoving aside the curtains, he heard hooves scattering gravel down the lane.

"Too late. He's gone."

"Are you sure?"

"Yep. By now, he's probably turned up The Pike." As Augie headed through the dark foyer toward the parlor, he ran straight into his father.

"Are you two alright?"

"No." His daughter collapsed onto the settee, shaking her head back and forth before thrusting it into her hands. "We just watched Hugh digging up Augie's treasure chest."

"Phoebe, it wasn't Hugh!"

"I'm telling you it was! I know his cape. I saw it just this week."

"Kitten, you are obviously distraught. Someone else may have grabbed it."

"Out of his dressing room?"

"Augie, why don't you sit down next to your sister and fill me in on the details. I want to make proper sense of what your sister is saying."

While he did as their father asked, they heard footsteps crossing the foyer. "Will you three please quiet down? You will wake up Lucy. Ernest, what has happened?"

While he briefly explained, Mama felt around for a parlor lamp and lit the wick. "This is all very upsetting, especially for you, Kitten, but your brother is right. Anyone who owns livestock is likely to have an oil skin, and from your bedroom window, who can say who was under that cape?"

"At least," added Phoebe, "It leaves out Clara."

Papa smoothed down the ends of his mustache. "Height is hard to judge from a distance."

"Clara—on the eve of her wedding—digging around in the mud?"

"I admit that is hard to imagine. Did you happen to see the person's skin?"

"Only for an instant, but I'm sure it was white. If it was dark, we wouldn't have been able to distinguish it."

"Well, I'd better saddle up Esmeralda and head up to The Lilacs."

"Oh, Ernest, you can't. Not at this hour. Tomorrow is Clara's big day."

"I must act quickly. How else will they see whose boots are muddy? Only a man with a very pressing reason would be out on a night like this."

"Which is exactly why you mustn't go. Do you think he will be foolish enough to track his wet clothes through Lavinia's parlor? He will rid himself of them in one of the outbuildings and be waiting for you when he hears a horse galloping."

"You think me a coward?"

"I think you are sensible."

"We all know how brave you are, Papa," added Phoebe. "But Mama does have a point."

"Of course, I do. The most you could say is our children saw a man in the park they can't identify. This horrible murder has ruined enough; let's not let it ruin Clara's wedding."

# Chapter 38

PHOEBE WENT TO the sanctuary early to ensure the nosegays they had tied to the pew ends still looked fresh. That accomplished, she knelt on an altar bench.

"Father, I would like to say thank You for Your very nature, for loving us so intimately. You know the end from the beginning, still, I just can't shake my unease about this marriage. Only You truly know for certain what's in Clara's heart or Lord Dunham's concerning You, but Lord, whether they are Yours or not, please in Your mercy prevent this wedding from taking place if it is not by Your design. I am also scared for Charles. For all Mr. Dyer's cleverness, he refuses all arguments to free him, though I remain as convinced as ever of his innocence. Even more pressing is the man we saw last night. I am just devastated to think it might be Hugh, and how am I to act when I see him today? Please help me to hold my suspicions loosely so that I may offer the fairness to him I would to anyone. But it looked so much like him, God! And then, Lord, there are Aaron and Jubal. Please keep them safe from all harm."

"Ahem."

Phoebe rose as she heard her mother clear her throat.

"I'm sorry to disturb you, but I do not have much time left to practice the arioso Lavinia asked me to play. It's

Bach, and I'm afraid my attempt at playing it yesterday was rather poor."

"I thought it sounded splendid."

"I've been praying for them also."

Phoebe froze, wondering who 'them' included. To her knowledge, Mama knew nothing of Aaron's endeavors, let alone Jubal's part in them. She was still not sure Augie was correct about Papa. Yes, he had gone to The Lilacs on the last two Sunday evenings, but he knew well what might happen if he was holding services there. Slaves were forbidden by law from assembling. "Do you mind if I listen?"

"By no means! I relish your presence. We see each other so much less frequently since you began working for Lavinia. Do you honestly feel I played it well? I do not want to embarrass the Kikers."

"You've no reason for concern, Mama. I will sit in the back row with Augie since you and Papa will be seated up front. Where is Lucy?"

"Ruby kindly volunteered to watch her for the morning."

"It is a shame neither she nor Kitch and Mitilde can come to the ceremony. They have known Clara her entire life."

"At least they will see her at the reception." Amelia shook her head. "I will never get used to kind people who claim to be Christian owning other human beings. It just isn't right, and yet they appear to have little awareness of that fact. Do the Kikers ever speak with you about it?"

Phoebe caught her lower lip between her teeth, she so badly wished to defend Lavinia. Yet, the less her mother knew, the less she would need to hide, particularly if

Augie's theory about Papa's Sunday evenings was correct. "I don't think we've discussed the issue since that first dinner in their home. You remember—it was shortly after we came to the valley. Oh, no—wait. You were still in Baltimore taking care of Grandma Ada at the time."

"I'm sure your father made no pretense of approving. As much as I'd love to talk more, I'd best run through the piece another time or two."

As her mother lay her fingertips to the keyboard, Phoebe lay her head against the back wall and closed her eyes. The arioso was lovely, absorbing her attention so that she did not notice anyone come in until she heard the nearby crack of someone's knees.

"It's only me, Honey." When Phoebe opened her eyes, Lavinia was squatting beside her. "I didn't mean to startle you. The leaves and berries turned out far prettier than I expected. You have outdone yourself, but why are you sitting all the way back here?"

"I promised to watch Augie."

"Oh fiddlesticks. Augie is old enough to watch himself. Besides, he'd far rather sit with Jeremiah. Come on. You are like another daughter to me. Join us in our family's pew."

So many thoughts flew through Phoebe's mind at once, she was not sure what showed on her face. She was grateful for Lavinia's care, but the last person she wanted to sit with was Hugh. "Thank you. Let me make sure it's alright with Mama."

Lavinia patted Phoebe's arm as she straightened. "I will miss Clara horribly which makes me doubly grateful that we see you almost daily."

Once Phoebe obtained her mother's permission, she opened the half door to the Kiker's box and stepped up into their pew. Already, the Nelsons, the Simmonses, the Wilsons, and the Whites were arriving, along with an assortment of shopkeepers and other townsfolk she had met at the ball.

"Is this seat taken?" Hugh smiled as he scooted into the space next to Phoebe.

"Good…morning." It was the only thing she managed to squeak out, making her feel like a simpleton.

"Are you tired? You seem less cheerful than usual."

"Yes. The storm woke me up. And you? Did you sleep well last evening?"

"I hardly slept at all. One of our cows decided to calve in the early hours of the morning, right at the beginning of the storm. I am grateful Father had the foresight to keep her in the barn."

"That is fortunate, else even with an *oilskin cape* you would be drenched."

Hugh either looked at her a little oddly or she imagined he did. "I was, believe me, and my boots are still covered in mud."

"Your mother cannot have liked you walking on her carpets in them."

"I learned from a young age never to do that. Oh. I almost forgot." He removed a sealed envelope from his frock coat. "Mother meant to bring this to you yesterday, but with all the wedding preparations, her mind has been everywhere all at once."

"From whom?" Taking it from his hand, she flipped it over. It was surprisingly thick and addressed in a hand she did not recognize. "It doesn't have a return address."

"Sari found it on the tray in the hall while she was cleaning. Our *new butler* denied it came in with the mail pouch."

Phoebe did not miss the emphasis he placed on Jubal's replacement or the spark of a shared secret in his warm, dark eyes. She smiled, appreciating all he conveyed with a simple tone and forgetting for an instant to be wary of him. Dropping her gaze to the bundle of papers in her hand, she sucked in a quick, sharp breath.

Hugh pinned her with a quizzical brow, but her mother had finished the prelude music and was beginning Bach's Arioso. As they and their gathered friends were rising from their seats, she pointed to the signature scrawled on the bottom of a letter, Richard Whitcomb Wilcox, and then pivoted to watch the bride and her father coming down the aisle. She could not tell if Clara was truly happy. After the fashion of Queen Victoria, a veil hid her face, but as she proceeded to the front of the church, no one could misread Lord Dunham's expression. It was angelic.

While her father opened the ceremony, Phoebe trapped the packet of papers beneath her folded hands atop her lap.

"Dearly beloved, we are gathered together here in the sight of…"

With difficulty, she kept her eyes fixed on the bride and groom. She was eager to learn what Whitcomb had written, but as she glanced across Hugh to Lavinia, she resolved to wait at least until the wedding sermon. Hoping to lessen the bundle's draw, she lay it on the pew cushion; but alas, an official looking document slid from between the pages. It was a marriage certificate with a name she recognized written in a beautiful hand across it's middle. Surreptitiously, she scooted the remainder of the contents apart to find a trail of bills or receipts, several articles about a woman's disappearance, and a daguerreotype of a young couple.

"Secondly, it was ordained for a remedy against sin…"

When Phoebe picked up the daguerreotype and peered at it more closely, her eyes grew as round as the woman's bonnet.

"…which holy estate these two persons present come now to be joined…"

The wife was Isabel, without her wig, as surely as if she were standing in front of them. Once Phoebe's eyes moved to the adoring husband, she sprang to her feet before she considered what she was doing. "Stop!"

# Chapter 39

LAVINIA RECOILED, HER eyes filling with shock and her mouth dropping open, while Phoebe clutched the back of their pew. Reverend Farrell simply stared, as if momentarily stupefied, and then stated: "I haven't come to that part."

The absurdity of the timing so struck her, she was seized by a virulent urge to giggle. She tamped it down and glanced over her shoulder at the sixty-odd pair of eyes riveted to her face. As her legs began to wobble, she hoped they—and the Kikers—would forgive her ill-mannered outburst.

Hugh lay his hand over hers. "Continue."

"Isabela's dying word wasn't Whitcomb—it was Wickham!"

"Phoebe." Her father looked incredulous. "This is neither the time nor place. We are in the middle of your friend's wed…"

Before he could finish, Megan had bolted off her seat. "The cruel man Isabela told us about."

"Sit down, Meg," hissed William, tugging her back onto the pew. "You're making a spectacle of yourself."

Emily popped up also, gaping from Megan to Phoebe. "How did we not know? She announced it clearly."

As all three friends turned toward Clara, who still stood with her father, she whipped back her veil and glared at Lord Dunham. "It was you?"

All the color drained from his face. Shoving Asa aside, he fled toward the center aisle, but Colonel Nelson was too quick for him. He stuck out a leg while Hugh, with surprising agility, bounded over the pew box to wrestle him to the ground. As women gasped and men sprang forward, Dyer rushed to Hugh's aid.

Lord Dunham spewed curses, contorting his beatific features while they hauled him to his feet. As he threatened them all with the wrath of England, Judge Pennybacker instructed a few local men to tie his lordship's hands securely and lead him away.

"Oh, my dear love!" Lavinia rushed to the front as Clara began to totter unsteadily. "You might have been his next victim!"

The judge searched for Phoebe who had plopped down on her pew, overcome with contrary emotions. "Young woman, I should like to know what you are holding." Sticking a hand inside his coat, he searched his chest pocket. "I don't seem to have my glasses. Mr. Dyer, get those papers from the girl and read them to me."

While Dyer approached Phoebe with an outstretched hand, her mother dashed to her side. "Please." Amelia addressed friends who had begun to pelt her with questions. "Give her a chance to catch her breath."

They swiveled their heads toward Dyer, who, after shuffling through the documents, panned the crowd for Megan. "Miss Simmons, what did you mean by 'the cruel man'?"

"Perhaps someone has told you of the books we were reading. We formed a club of sorts to divert…I do not know what to call her."

"According to these records her given name was Genevieve, but what does this man have to do with Lord Dunham?"

"She said…he was…"

While Megan stumbled to answer, Mary Nelson cut in. "Jane Austen wrote a character into her novel 'Pride and Prejudice' that quite resembled Mr. Pinder. His appearance was guileless, and he spoke to everyone exactly what they wanted to hear, but underneath his charming veneer, he was cunning and cruel—not caring who he ruined. While the young women present contrasted the books' heroes, Isabela…or I guess I should call her Genevieve…cautioned them to look deeper than appearances."

"Can you recall her precise words?"

Mama Nelson glanced at Phoebe.

"'The most charming man I have known was also the cruelest.'"

Pastor Farrell held up his hand. "May I ask how that envelope came into the possession of my daughter?"

Asa Kiker answered. "We received it addressed to her at The Lilacs, so Hugh brought it for her this morning. Who is it from?"

Mr. Dyer flipped over the first page of the note to Phoebe, scanning for the signature. "Richard Whitcomb Wilcox. It seems, Miss Farrell, you made an impression on him. Do you mind if I read it aloud?"

When she shook her head, he continued. "'My Dear'—and so forth, 'I realize you regard my conduct as abominable, and since Asa Kiker banned me from his property, I now have no means to make an appeal. I know also I have risen to chief among the list of suspects as they are deeply digging into my background.'"

Dyer locked gazes with Asa. "He is correct. I asked you to keep Simmons under guard in hopes of lulling Whitcomb into a sense of ease. To continue: 'I trust when you receive this, you will put that good head that sits atop your shoulders to use. Genevieve Pinder's brother, in fear for her life, commissioned me to find her or, failing that, to prove her husband guilty of her murder.'"

Colonel Nelson cleared his throat. "Have you discovered anything about him—this brother: who he is and where he lives? We always did wonder."

"Yes, just yesterday. In a town by the name of Staunton. Mr. Kiker informs me it lies south of us."

"That would explain why she ended up on the parsonage doorstep and some of the questions she had asked Mary, Emily, and me."

"'As you peruse these documents,'" Dyer read, "'you will learn why I forced you into the garden that afternoon. Pinder had caught wind of my snooping and knew I would soon expose him. I was awaiting only one more piece of evidence from my assistant in London—the marriage certificate which I trust is now in the possession of your stone-faced admirer.'"

Dyer kept his eyes fixed to the page, though his ears turned crimson.

"'My banishment from The Lilacs has worked in my favor as it gave me freedom to assemble and post the enclosed without apprehension. However, since my own safety is now in jeopardy, I must entrust them to you. Yours truly, Richard Whitcomb Wilcox.'" Dyer offered the daguerreotype to the Nelsons. "There is no question the groom is Lord Dunham. Can you identify your houseguest?"

"It's her!" Mary's eyes opened wide. "I would know that face anywhere."

"And you, Colonel?"

"I am afraid so."

"Then Miss Kiker, you are a very fortunate young woman."

Lavinia and Asa were leading her down the aisle she had walked up not half an hour previously, when her father stopped. "We are going home and would like to invite each of you to join us. What would have been Clara's wedding breakfast will now be a celebration of her rescue." He smiled pointedly at Phoebe.

As each family crossed through the foyer into the churchyard, they boarded carriages and wagons. A few, Mr. Dyer among them, mounted horses.

"Will you," asked the reverend, "return to The Lilacs or travel to Staunton in search of…Genevieve's brother?"

"If you permit me, I will accompany your family. I have questions yet to ask Phoebe."

Augie squinted up at the investigator. "And boy, do we have a story to tell you."

***

ALL THE WAY along and past the Simmonses' property, Augie engaged Mr. Dyer in his tale of their storm-drenched digger, concluding with his sister's ridiculous supposition it was Hugh.

Dyer locked eyes with Phoebe. "Not ridiculous at all. It was exactly what Lord Dunham wanted anyone who saw him to think. In fact, he waited until Hugh went into the barn to slip into his room and grab his oilskin."

"Hugh did not wear it?"

"He had no need to, at least not yet. It was raining lightly when the poor animal began showing signs of distress."

"But," began Phoebe, "how do you know all this?"

"After Spry botched his attempt to trail Whitcomb, I had no recourse but to watch and follow Pinder myself. And unlike Whitcomb, he hadn't a clue."

Augie frowned and cocked his head. "Why did he steal my chest, and when will I get it back?"

"Today, providing Judge Pennybacker agrees. Yesterday morning at breakfast, I let it slip that you had found something interesting buried in the hole of your treasure chest—a trinket of some sort. Although the entire table showed interest, only Pinder asked me what you had done with your find."

"And…" Augie gestured for him to continue.

"I told him you'd done what any energetic and intelligent boy would likely do with found treasure."

"So, he assumed my brother had returned it to the box."

"Just so. Before you received those documents from Whitcomb—or I guess we should say Wilcox—I hadn't any proof of what he'd done."

"When," asked the reverend, "did you begin to suspect him?"

"At their engagement party the first night I arrived. I'd already discovered his itinerary while interviewing Wilcox. It didn't square with his hasty return to England."

"But how did you know you could trust what Whit…Wilcox said?"

"I didn't, but the contradiction caught my attention. I wasn't sure of anything until I followed Pinder to the parsonage."

Phoebe looked awash with concern. "Were you just going to let Clara marry him?"

"No. I had planned to apprehend him before the ceremony, but when I saw that packet of papers with your name on it, I endeavored to intercept them. Your young Mr. Kiker refused me. Had you not stood up when you did, I would have been forced—at the proper time—to do so."

"What about Charles?"

"You never believed him guilty."

"Nor did anyone who knew him, but why did he leave The Lilacs that evening?"

"Your brother was on to the correct scent when he said Clara could not have lifted Charles onto a horse. I suppose Pinder knocked him out before he…killed…the woman we now know was his wife. Then he likely pulled off and planted that button himself, tossed Charles across his horse, and gave it a good whack. I am not much of a horseman, but I assume it knew its way home."

Augie twisted on his seat. "How about William? Who had been pestering him?"

"Lord Dunham is undoubtedly the man his sisters called Gabriel."

"Of course," muttered Phoebe, "after the angel."

"No one would call Whitcomb by that name, though I will not be surprised to learn he was the man who tried to hire William. He astutely trailed her from one side of the Atlantic to the other."

Augie scrambled onto his knees. "You think Mr. Pinder killed him?"

"You'd better sit down, son," his father interrupted, "lest you tumble out. We all have questions, but now that we have arrived, the answers will need to wait. We don't want to put the Kikers through any more of an ordeal than they have endured already."

# Chapter 40

AS THE FARRELLS and Mr. Dyer drove up to The Lilacs' front door, Clara, who had just exited her family's carriage, squealed. "Charles!" Gathering up her wedding gown she ran straight for the front steps and into the arms of the man she loved.

"How did he get free?" asked Amelia. "I thought he was still a suspect."

"I set him loose this morning and imagine, by now, he has heard the news."

"I don't know if I've ever seen Clara so happy. She now has two things to celebrate, though I'm not sure Lavinia and Asa will feel the same."

"We'll soon find out," replied her husband. "Young man, if our small town could find sufficient funds to pay you, would you consider moving to this valley? From what I have seen, the only lawman we have is Spry, and he is no lawman at all."

"I doubt you have enough crime to keep me busy."

"I'm not so sure of that," exclaimed Amelia. "This is our second murder. We've only lived here eighteen months."

The reverend climbed from the wagon. "I'm sorry. We shouldn't put you on the spot."

Dyer raised one brow as he assisted Phoebe. "The idea does hold some attractions, but I'm more inclined toward a city life. During the past week, I've ridden more than I did all year, and I have the soreness to prove it."

"Well, while my daughter tries to talk you into staying, her mother and I will go inside. Come, Augie. I think I see Jeremiah." While he, his wife and his son ascended the tall porch steps, Mr. Dyer folded his hands behind his back.

"Miss Farrell, would you like to take a turn around the garden?"

"Won't you be wanted inside? I would imagine Judge Pennybacker will have questions for you."

His eyes lit as they met hers. "They can wait, and your father had a point: the Kikers need a reprieve."

"When will you return to Allentown?"

"This evening if I can find room on the train. That distance on a horse is out of the question."

"I am sure Matthew Bentley will be glad to see you."

"Do you plan to visit them soon?"

"No. Although I like both him and Tandy, we do not know each other well enough for them to issue that sort of invitation."

He offered her a hint of a smile. "It is their loss—and mine."

"Phoebe!" Virginia ran to the edge of the porch. "Come quick. Charles has just asked Mr. Kiker for Clara's hand."

"He wasted no time."

Once the two of them slipped inside the house, they found Reverend Farrell framed with his back to the huge double windows that opened onto to the patio. Before him stood Clara and Charles, their hands locked together. "As Mr. and Mrs. Kiker have consented, we're going to have a wedding after all."

# Meet the Author

Sydney Tooman Betts resides with her husband near the extensive cavern system that inspired the setting for several chapters in her series The People of the Book.

While single, Ms. Betts (B.S. Bible/Missiology, M. Ed) took part in a variety of cross-cultural adventures in North and Central America. After marrying, she and her husband lived in Europe and the Middle East where he served in various mission-support capacities. Her teaching experiences span preschool to guest lecturing at the graduate level.

Before penning her first novel, *A River too Deep,* she ghost-wrote several stories for an adult literacy program.

# Dear Reader,

I have discovered a pitfall inherent to a mystery series where many of the characters are and will stay interconnected. How do I portray the realistic effects a prior mystery would have had on a character without spoiling it for readers who picked up the books out of order? For example, Clara asks her mother why her father has begun to treat Charles differently than he did at one time. Her mother skirts her question. Why? She—and in a later discussion, Hugh and Phoebe—cannot answer without divulging another character's confidences and revealing the ending of Phoebe's Secret.

Is this fair? It would not be if the information offered a clue to solve this book's mystery. However, it does not. It only offers a further peek into Clara and Charles's hearts and frustrations. Therefore, in lieu of an explanation, I have inserted an endnote to let you know where you can satisfy your curiosity.

By now, you may have guessed one or more characters are involved with the Underground Railroad. Which ones they are, I will leave you to discover along with our heroine, and hope you have fun gathering hints along the way.

All names employed throughout the book are historically accurate, whether the character is enslaved or free, but *Phoebe's Mysteries* are wholly works of fiction. I have loosely based The Lilacs on a plantation in the Shenandoah Valley and occasionally include historical figures. Beyond those, each character is a product of my imagination except for a few portrayals, by name and with permission, of beloved friends.

Writing is far easier and more pleasant than marketing, so please consider leaving a rating or honest review on Goodreads, Amazon, or any other site where you purchased this novel. I am deeply grateful for your efforts. They make a huge difference.

Lastly, you have been getting to know me through these pages. I would enjoy getting to know you. If you would like to know more about me, my books, or most importantly, Jesus, please visit my Facebook author page.

I am sincerely grateful for your constant encouragement, love and support. You have kept my head up when it was drooping and pushed me to become a better writer.

Your friendship is a true reward!

*Sydney*

# Endnotes

[i] Phoebe's Secret
[ii] John 2:24-25
[iii] 1st Corinthians 13:7
[iv] Jane Austen, Pride and Prejudice (Barnes and Noble Classics), p. 9
[v] Ibid., p. 9
[vi] Romans 5:8
[vii] Philippians 2:8
[viii] Acts 18
[ix] See Author's Note
[x] Jane Austen, Pride and Prejudice, p. 1
[xi] See Phoebe's Secret
[xii] See Phoebe's Secret
[xiii] See Author's Note
[xiv] Jane Austen, Pride and Prejudice, p. 179
[xv] Jane Austen, Pride and Prejudice, p. 66
[xvi] I Peter 4:12
[xvii] See Phoebe's Christmas

Made in the USA
Middletown, DE
07 October 2021

49604780R00144